MR. GWYN

&

THREE TIMES AT DAWN

MR. GWYN

&

THREE TIMES AT DAWN

ALESSANDRO BARICCO

TRANSLATED BY
ANN GOLDSTEIN

McSWEENEY'S
SAN FRANCISCO

McSWEENEY'S
SAN FRANCISCO

McSweeney's and colophon are registered trademarks of McSweeney's, a privately held company with wildly fluctuating resources.

Printed in Michigan by Thomson-Shore.

ISBN: 978-1-938073-96-0

www.mcsweeneys.net

MR.
GWYN

1.

As he was walking through Regent's Park—along the path he always chose, among the many—Jasper Gwyn suddenly had the clear sensation that what he had been doing every day to earn his living no longer suited him. This thought had surfaced several times already, but never with such clarity and so much grace.

So when he got home he began writing an article, which he then printed out, put in an envelope, and, crossing the city, delivered personally to the editorial offices of the *Guardian*. He was known there. Occasionally he contributed to the paper. He asked if it was possible to wait a week before publishing it.

The article consisted of a list of fifty-two things that Jasper Gwyn intended never to do again. The first was to write articles for the *Guardian*. The thirteenth was to meet students and pretend to be sure of himself. The thirty-first, to be photographed with his hand on his chin, looking thoughtful. The forty-seventh, to make an effort to be cordial to colleagues whom he in truth despised. The last was: to write books. In a certain sense he was closing the possible loophole that the penultimate might have left: to publish books.

It should be said that at that time Jasper Gwyn was a writer, quite fashionable in England and fairly well known abroad. He had made his debut twelve years earlier, with a thriller set in the Welsh countryside in the era of Thatcherism: a case of mysterious disappearances. Three years later, he had published a short novel about two sisters who decide never to see each other again: for a hundred pages they try to realize their modest desire, but it turns out to be impossible. The book ended with an extraordinary scene on a pier, in winter. Apart from an essay on Chesterton and two stories published in different anthologies, the oeuvre of Jasper Gwyn concluded with a third novel, five hundred pages long. It was the tranquil confession of an old Olympic fencing champion, a former navy captain and radio variety-show host. It was written in the first person and entitled *Lights Off*. It began with this sentence: "I have often reflected on sowing and reaping."

As many had noted, the three novels were so different from one another that it was difficult to recognize them as products of the same hand. It was an odd phenomenon, but it hadn't kept Jasper Gwyn from becoming, in a short time, a writer acclaimed by the public and generally respected by the critics. His talent for storytelling was certainly indisputable, and in particular the ease with which he was able to identify with his characters and re-create their feelings was disconcerting. He seemed to know the words that they would say, and to think their thoughts, before they did. It's not surprising if to many, in those years, it seemed reasonable to predict for him a brilliant career.

At the age of forty-three, however, Jasper Gwyn wrote an article for the *Guardian* in which he listed fifty-two things that, starting that day, he would never do again. And the last was: write books.

His brilliant career was already over.

2.

The morning the article in the *Guardian* came out—with a big headline, in the Sunday supplement—Jasper Gwyn was in Spain, in Granada: it seemed to him appropriate, in the circumstances, to put a certain distance between himself and the world. He had chosen a hotel so modest that there was no telephone in the room, and so that morning someone had to come up to inform him that there was a call for him downstairs in the lobby. He went down in his pajamas and reluctantly went over to an old telephone, painted yellow, placed on a wicker table. He leaned the receiver against his ear and what he heard was the voice of Tom Bruce Shepperd, his agent.

"What's this all about, Jasper?"

"What's what about?"

"The fifty-two things. I read them this morning, Lottie gave me the paper, I was still in bed. I practically had a stroke."

"Maybe I should have warned you."

"You're not telling me it's serious. Is it a challenge, a statement, what the hell is it?"

"Nothing, an article. But it's all true."

"In what sense?"

"I mean I wrote it seriously. It's exactly what I've decided."

"You're telling me you're going to stop writing?"

"Yes."

"You're crazy."

"I really have to go, you know?"

"Wait a second, Jasper, we've got to talk about it, if you don't talk about it to me, your agent…"

"There's nothing to add, I'm going to stop writing and that's it."

"You know something, Jasper, are you listening to me, you know something?"

"Yes, I'm listening to you."

"Then listen to me, I've heard that statement dozens of times, I've heard it said by an unimaginable number of writers, I've even heard Martin Amis say it, do you believe me? It must have been ten years ago, Martin Amis said those exact words, I'm going to stop writing, and it's only one example, but I could give you twenty, you want me to make you a list?"

"I don't think it's necessary."

"And you know something? Not one of them really stopped, there's no such thing as stopping."

"Okay, but now I really have to go, Tom."

"Not one."

"Okay."

"Good article, anyway."

"Thank you."

"You've really thrown a stone in the pond."

"Don't use that expression, please."

"What?"

"Nothing. Now I'm going."

"I'm expecting you in London, when are you coming? Lottie

would be really happy to see you."

"I'm about to hang up, Tom."

"Jasper, big brother, don't joke."

"I've hung up, Tom."

He spoke that last sentence, however, after he hung up, so Tom Bruce Shepperd didn't hear it.

3.

Jasper Gwyn stayed in the Spanish hotel, comfortably, for sixty-two days. When he paid the bill, his extra expenses included seventy-two cups of cold milk, seventy-two glasses of whiskey, two phone calls, an exorbitant laundry bill (129 items), and the purchase price of a transistor radio—which may throw some light on his inclinations.

During his entire sojourn in Granada, given the distance, and the isolation, Jasper Gwyn didn't have to return to the subject of his article except occasionally, in his own mind. One day, however, he happened to meet a young Slovenian woman and he ended up having a pleasant conversation with her in the courtyard garden of a museum. She was brilliant and self-assured, and she spoke fairly good English. She said that she worked at the University of Ljubljana, in the Department of Modern and Contemporary History. She was in Spain to do research: she was working on the history of an Italian noblewoman who, at the end of the nineteenth century, traveled around Europe looking for relics.

"You know, trafficking in relics, at the time, was the hobby of a certain Catholic aristocracy," she explained.

"Really?"

"It's not well known, but it's a fascinating story."

"Tell me."

They dined together, and at dessert, after discoursing at length about the tibias and phalanges of martyrs, the Slovenian woman began to talk about herself, and in particular of how lucky she felt to be a researcher, a profession that she considered wonderful. She added that, naturally, everything surrounding the profession was horrible, the colleagues, the competition, the mediocrity, the hypocrisy—everything. But she also said that as far as she was concerned absolutely nothing could take away the desire to study and write.

"I'm happy to hear you say that," Jasper Gwyn commented.

Then the woman asked what he did. Jasper Gwyn hesitated a moment, and then he half-lied. He said that for a dozen years he had been an interior designer, but two weeks ago he had stopped. The woman appeared to be sorry about it and asked why he had given up a job that seemed so enjoyable. Jasper Gwyn gestured vaguely in the air. Then he said something incomprehensible.

"One day I realized that nothing mattered to me anymore, and that everything was like a fatal wound."

The woman appeared to be intrigued, but Jasper Gwyn was skilled at leading the conversation to other subjects, slipping sidewise into the custom of putting a carpet in the bathroom, and then expatiating on the supremacy of southern civilizations, due to their knowledge of the exact meaning of the term *light*.

Much later that evening they said good night, but they did it so slowly that the young Slovenian woman had time to find the right words to say that it would be nice to spend that night together.

Jasper Gwyn wasn't so sure about it, but he followed her to her hotel room. Then, mysteriously, it wasn't so complicated to mix her haste and his caution in a Spanish bed.

Two days later, when the Slovenian woman left, Jasper Gwyn gave her a list he had compiled of thirteen brands of Scotch whiskey.

"What are they?" she asked.

"Lovely names. I'm giving them to you."

Jasper Gwyn spent sixteen more days in Granada. Then he, too, left, forgetting in the hotel three shirts, an unpaired sock, a walking stick with an ivory head, a sandalwood bubble bath, and two telephone numbers written in felt-tipped pen on the plastic shower curtain.

4.

Jasper Gwyn spent the first days of his return to London walking the streets of the city obsessively and for long periods, with the delightful conviction that he had become invisible. Since he had stopped writing, in his mind he had stopped being a public figure— there was no reason for people to notice him, now that he was an ordinary person again. He began dressing carelessly, and went back to doing many small things without the subconscious thought that he ought to be presentable, in case a reader suddenly recognized him. The position he took at the bar in the pub, for example. Riding the bus without a ticket. Eating by himself at McDonald's. Every so often someone did recognize him, and then he denied that he was who he was.

There were a lot of other things he no longer had to deal with. He was like one of those horses who, having shaken off the jockey, slow down, dreamily, to a gentle trot, while the others are still bursting their lungs in pursuit of a finish line and an order of arrival. That state of mind was infinitely pleasurable. When he happened upon an article in the newspaper or a bookshop window that reminded him of the fray he had just withdrawn from, he felt his heart grow light, and he breathed the childish intoxication of Saturday afternoon. It was years since he had felt so good.

Partly for this reason he put off for a while taking the measure of his new life, prolonging that private atmosphere of vacation. The idea, developed during his sojourn in Spain, was to return to the profession he had had before publishing novels. It wouldn't be difficult, or even unpleasant. One might perhaps see a certain formal elegance, a sort of strophic progress, as in a ballad. Nothing, however, pressed him to hurry that return, since Jasper Gwyn lived alone, and had no family and few expenses, and thus, for at least a couple of years, he could live in tranquility without even getting up in the morning. So he put the thing off, and devoted himself to casual acts and to tasks that he had long postponed.

He threw away old newspapers. He took trains for unknown destinations.

5.

What happened, however, was that, as the days passed, he discovered in himself a singular form of unease that he had trouble understanding and that only after a while did he come to recognize: although it was vexing to admit it, he missed the act of writing, and the daily care of ordering thoughts into the rectilinear form of a sentence. He hadn't expected it, and this caused him to reflect. It was a sort of small irritation that showed up every day and promised to get worse. So, little by little, Jasper Gwyn began to wonder if he shouldn't consider marginal jobs in which it would be possible for him to pursue the practice of writing without its necessitating an immediate return to the fifty-two things he had vowed never to do again.

Travel guides, he said to himself. But he would have to travel.

He thought of writers of instruction manuals for household appliances, and wondered if there still existed, somewhere in the world, the job of writing letters for those who were unable to do it.

Translator, he thought. But from what language?

In the end, the only thing that came clearly to mind was a word: *copyist*. He would like to be a copyist. It wasn't a real profession, he realized, but the word had a resonance that was convincing, and inspired him to look for something precise. There was a secrecy in the act, and a patience in its methods—a mixture of modesty and solemnity. He would not like to do anything but that: be a copyist. He was sure that he could do it well.

As he tried to imagine what in the real world might correspond to the word *copyist*, Jasper Gwyn let a lot of days slip by, one after another, apparently painlessly. He was scarcely aware of them.

6.

Every so often contracts arrived for him to sign, which had to do with the books he had already written. Renewals, new translations, adaptations for the theater. He left them on the table, and in the end it was clear to him that he would never sign them. With some distress he discovered that not only did he no longer want to write books but, in some way, he didn't even want to have written them. That is, he had liked doing it but he didn't want them to have survived his decision to stop, and in fact it bothered him that, with a force of their own, they went where he had promised himself never to set foot again. He began to throw away the contracts without even opening them. Every so often Tom passed on letters from admirers who politely thanked him for such and such a page, or a particular story. Even that made him nervous, and he noticed that none of them mentioned his silence—they didn't seem to be informed about it. A couple of times he took the trouble to answer. He thanked them, in turn, with simple words. Then he added that he had stopped writing, and signed off.

He noted that no one answered those letters.

More and more often, however, that need to write returned, and he missed the daily care with which he put his thoughts in order, in the straight line of a sentence. Instinctively, then, he ended up compensating for that absence with a private liturgy, which did not seem to him without some beauty: he began to write *mentally*, while he was walking, or lying in bed with the light out, waiting for sleep. He chose words, he constructed sentences. He might follow an idea for days, writing in his head entire pages, which he then enjoyed repeating, sometimes aloud. He could, in the same way, have cracked his knuckles, or practiced athletic exercises, over and over again. It was a physical thing. He liked it.

Once he wrote, in that way, an entire poker game. One of the players was a child.

In particular he liked to write while he was waiting at the Laundromat, amid the spinning drums, to the rhythm of magazines leafed through distractedly on the crossed legs of women who did not seem to harbor any illusions that did not concern the slenderness of their ankles. One day he was writing in his mind a dialogue between two lovers in which the man was explaining that ever since he was a child he had had the curious faculty of dreaming about people only when he was sleeping with them, only *while* he was sleeping with them.

"You mean that you only dream about people who are in your bed?" the woman asked.

"Yes."

"What sort of nonsense is that?"

"I don't know."

"And if someone isn't in your bed you don't dream about her."

"Never."

At that point a fat, rather elegant girl came up to him, there in the Laundromat, and she handed him a cell phone.

"It's for you," she said.

Jasper Gwyn took the phone.

7.

"Jasper! Did you put in the fabric softener?"

"Hello, Tom."

"Am I disturbing you?"

"I was writing."

"Bingo!"

"Not in that sense."

"I don't find that there are many senses, if someone is a writer he writes, that's it. I told you, no one really succeeds in stopping."

"Tom, I'm in the Laundromat."

"I know, you're always there. And at home you don't answer."

"Books aren't written in a Laundromat, you know, and anyway I wouldn't write them."

"Bullshit. Come clean. What is it, a story?"

The laundry was still in prewash, and there was no one leafing through magazines. So Jasper Gwyn thought he could try to explain. He told Tom Bruce Shepperd that he liked lining up words, and forming sentences, the way he might crack his knuckles. He did it in the closed space of his mind. It relaxed him.

"Fantastic! I'll come there, you speak, I record, and the book is done. You wouldn't be the first to use a system like that."

Jasper Gwyn explained to him that they weren't even stories, they were fragments, without a before and without an after—really, they could hardly even be called scenes.

"Brilliant. I've already got the title."

"Don't tell me."

"*Scenes from Books that I Will Never Write.*"

"You told me."

"Don't move, I have to take care of two things and I'll be there."

"Tom."

"Tell me, brother."

"Who is this elegant girl here?"

"Rebecca? She's new, very good."

"What does she do besides carry around a cell phone in Laundromats?"

"She's learning, you have to begin somewhere."

Jasper Gwyn thought that if there was one thing he didn't like about having stopped being a writer it was that he would no longer have any reason to work with Tom Bruce Shepperd. He thought that one day Tom would stop following him around with his phone calls, and that would be a bad day. He wondered if it wouldn't be right to tell him. There, in the Laundromat. Then he had a better idea.

He closed the phone and nodded to the fat girl, who had moved a few steps away, out of politeness. He noticed that she had a very beautiful face, and, besides, she limited the damage by choosing her clothes well. He asked her if he could give her a message for Tom.

"Of course."

"Be so kind then as to tell him that I miss him."

"Of course."

"I mean that sooner or later he'll stop bothering me wherever I go, and I'll feel the same relief you feel when you're in a room and the refrigerator motor stops, but also the same inevitable dismay, and the sensation, which you surely know, of not being certain what to do with that sudden silence, and maybe not, ultimately, being equal to it. Do you think you understand?"

"I'm not sure."

"Would you like me to repeat it?"

"Maybe I should take notes."

Jasper Gwyn shook his head. Too complicated, he thought. He opened the phone again. Tom's voice arrived. Exactly how those gadgets functioned he would never understand.

"Tom, be quiet a second."

"Jasper?"

"I want to tell you something."

"Shoot."

He told him. About the business of the refrigerator and all the rest. Tom Bruce Shepperd coughed and was silent for a few seconds, something he never did.

The girl then went off, walking in that slightly ship-like way that fat people have of walking, but first she smiled at Jasper Gwyn as she said goodbye, with a radiant light in her eyes, with her magnificent lips, her white teeth.

8.

Yet winter seemed pointlessly long that year, and the fact that he woke up early in the morning, sleepless, in darkness, began to offend him.

One day, when it was cold and raining, he was sitting in the waiting room of a clinic, a number in his hand. He had persuaded the doctor to prescribe some tests—he claimed he didn't feel well. A woman with a full shopping cart and a soaking-wet umbrella that kept falling down came and sat beside him. An old woman, with a rain scarf on her head. She took it off at some point, and in the way she smoothed her hair there was something like the remains of a seduction interrupted many years earlier. The umbrella, however, continued to fall in every direction.

"May I help you?" asked Jasper Gwyn.

The woman looked at him, then said that they ought to have umbrella stands in the clinics on rainy days. Someone, she added, had only to remove it when the sun returned.

"It's a sensible argument," said Jasper Gwyn.

"Of course it is," said the woman.

Then she took the umbrella and laid it down on the floor. It seemed like an arrow, or the edge of something. Slowly a puddle of water formed around it.

"Are you Jasper Gwyn or just someone who looks like him?" the woman asked. She did it as she searched for something small in her purse. As her hands rummaged in it she looked up to be sure that he had heard the question.

Jasper Gwyn wasn't expecting it, so he said yes, he was Jasper Gwyn.

"Bravo," said the woman, as if he had answered a quiz question correctly. Then she said that the scene on the wharf, in *Sisters*, was the best thing she had read in recent years.

"Thank you," said Jasper Gwyn.

"And also the fire in the school, at the beginning of the other book, the long one, the fire in the school is perfect."

Again she looked up at Jasper Gwyn.

"I was a teacher," she explained.

Then she took two candies out of her purse, they were round, citrus-flavored, and offered one to Jasper Gwyn.

"Thank you, no, really," he said.

"Come on!" she said.

He smiled and took the candy.

"The fact that they're lying in the bottom of my purse doesn't mean they're disgusting," she said.

"No, of course not."

"But I've noticed that people tend to think so."

Jasper Gwyn thought it was just like that, people are suspicious of a candy found at the bottom of a purse.

"I think it's the same phenomenon that causes people to be always slightly distrustful of orphans," he said.

The woman turned to look at him, astonished.

"Or the last car in the Tube," she said, with a strange happiness in her voice.

They were like two people who had been at school together as children, and now were reeling off the names of their classmates, bringing them back from enormous distances. A moment of silence passed between them, like a spell.

Then they began talking, and when a nurse came and announced that it was Mr. Gwyn's turn, Jasper Gwyn said he couldn't right then.

"You'll lose your turn," the nurse said.

"It doesn't matter. I can come back tomorrow."

"As you wish," the nurse said coldly. Then in a loud voice she called a Mr. Flewer.

The thing seemed totally normal to the woman with the umbrella.

In the end they found themselves alone in the waiting room, and then the woman said that it was really time to go. Jasper Gwyn asked if she didn't have to have a test, or something like that. But she said that she came there because it was a warm place, and it was exactly halfway between her house and the supermarket. Besides, she liked looking at the faces of people who had to have blood tests, and hadn't eaten anything. They seem like people who've been robbed of something, she said. Yes, Jasper Gwyn confirmed, convinced.

He took her home, holding the umbrella open over her, as she didn't want to give up the cart, and on the way they continued to talk until the woman asked what he was writing now, and he said Nothing. The woman walked for a while in silence, then she said, "A pity." She said it in a tone of regret so sincere that Jasper Gwyn was grieved by it.

"No more ideas?" the woman asked.

"No, it's not that."

"Then what?"

"I'd like to have another profession."

"Like?"

Jasper Gwyn stopped.

"I think I'd like to be a copyist."

The woman thought for a bit. Then she started walking again.

"Yes, I can understand," she said.

"Really?"

"Yes. It's a fine profession, copyist."

"That's what I thought."

"It's a *clean* profession," she said.

They said goodbye on the steps that led to her house, and to neither of them did it occur to exchange telephone numbers or mention a next time. Only she said that she was sorry to learn that she wouldn't read any more books by him. She added that not everyone is capable of entering into people's heads the way he could, and that it would be a pity to lock up that talent in the garage and polish it once a year, like a vintage sports car.

She said just that, "like a vintage sports car." Then she seemed to have finished, but in fact she still had something left.

"Being a copyist has to do with copying something, doesn't it?" she asked.

"Probably."

"There. But not legal documents or numbers, please."

"I'll try to avoid it."

"See if you find something like copying people."

"Yes."

"How they're made."

"Yes."

"You'll see them well."

"Yes."

9.

Perhaps a year, a year and a half, had passed since the article in the *Guardian*, when Jasper Gwyn began to feel ill, from time to time, in a way that he would describe as a sudden vanishing. He would see himself from the outside—so he related—or rather he lost every accurate perception that was not perception itself. At times it could be terrible. One day he had to go into a telephone booth and with a great effort dialed Tom's number. He said, stammering, that he no longer knew where he was.

"Don't worry, I'll send Rebecca to get you. Where are you?"

"That's the problem, Tom."

In the end the fat girl drove around the whole neighborhood until she found him. In the meantime Jasper Gwyn had stayed in the booth, spasmodically clutching the receiver and trying not to die. To distract himself he talked on the telephone—he improvised a phone call to protest the cutting off of the aqueduct, no one had informed him and it had caused enormous damage, economic and moral. He kept repeating, "Do I have to wait until it rains to shampoo my hair?"

He immediately felt better, as soon as he got into the fat girl's car.

While he apologized, he couldn't stop staring at the fat hands that gripped—but the verb wasn't exact—the sporty steering wheel. There was no coherence, he thought, and that must be the experience that at every instant of the day the girl had of her own body—that there was no coherence between it and all the rest.

But she smiled her lovely smile and said that in fact she was honored to be able to help him. And anyway, she added, it had happened to her, too, she had had a period when she was often ill in that way.

"All of a sudden you thought you were dying?"

"Yes."

"And how did you get better?" asked Jasper Gwyn, who at that point would have begged for a cure from anyone.

The girl smiled again, then she was silent, looking at the street.

"No," she said finally, "that's my business."

"Of course," said Jasper Gwyn.

They rolled. Probably that was the right verb. They rolled around the steering wheel.

10.

In the days that followed, Jasper Gwyn tried to stay calm, and in the attempt to find a salve for the crises, which were becoming more and more frequent, he relied on an exercise that he recalled seeing in a film. It consisted of living slowly, concentrating on every single gesture. As a rule it might seem rather vague, but Jasper Gwyn had a way of observing it that made it surprisingly concrete. So when he put on his shoes he looked at them first, assessing their fine lightness and appreciating the softness of the leather. As he laced them he avoided lapsing into an automatic action and examined in detail the splendid movement of his fingers, with a rounded gesture whose assurance he admired. Then he stood up, and at the first steps he made sure to register the solid grip of the shoe on the instep. In the same way, he concentrated on noises that are usually taken for granted, hearing again the click of a lock, the hoarseness of tape, or the faintest clatter of hinges. Much time was given to registering colors, even when the object had no usefulness, and in particular he was careful to admire the random palettes produced by the placement of things—whether it was the inside of a drawer, or the area of a parking lot. Often he counted the objects he came across—steps, streetlights, shouts—and with his fingers he checked surfaces, rediscovering the infinite range between rough and smooth. He stopped to look at shadows on the ground. He felt every coin between his fingers.

All this gave a luxurious rhythm to his daily movements, like those of an actor, or an African animal. Others seemed to recognize in his elegant slowness the natural tempo of things; and in the precision of his gestures a dominion over objects that most had forgotten returned to the surface. Jasper Gwyn wasn't even aware of it, and yet it was very clear to him that that meticulous pacing restored to him some solidity—that center of gravity which had evidently failed.

11.

It lasted a couple of months. Then, weary, he returned to normal living, but right away the familiar sensation of vanishing gripped him, and he was defenseless against the incurable feeling of emptiness that assailed him. Besides, that obsessive care in approaching the world—that way of tying his shoes—wasn't, after all, very different from *writing* things rather than *living* them, from lingering over adjectives and adverbs, and so Jasper Gwyn had to admit to himself that abandoning books had produced an emptiness that he didn't know how to remedy except by practicing imperfect and provisional substitute liturgies, like putting sentences together in his mind or tying his shoes at an idiotically slow pace. It had taken years to admit that the profession of writer had become impossible for him, and now he found himself forced to register that without that profession it was very difficult for him to go on. So in the end he realized that he was in a situation known to many humans, but not therefore less painful: that which alone makes them feel alive is something that is, slowly, fated to kill them. Children, for parents; success, for artists; mountains too high, for mountain climbers. Writing books, for Jasper Gwyn.

Realizing this made him feel lost, and helpless the way only children are, the intelligent ones. He was surprised to feel an instinct that wasn't habitual with him, something like the urgent necessity to talk to someone. He thought about it for a while, but the only person who came to mind was the old woman with the rain scarf, in the clinic. It would be much more natural to talk to Tom, he knew, and for a moment it even seemed possible to ask for help, in some way, from one of the women who had loved him, and who certainly would be delighted to listen to him. But the truth is that the only person with whom he really would have liked to talk about the matter was the old woman in the clinic: her, her umbrella, and her rain scarf. He was sure she would understand. So in the end Jasper Gwyn had other tests prescribed—it wasn't hard, on the basis of his symptoms—and he went back to the waiting room where he had met her that day.

In the hours that he spent there, waiting for her, during the three days of the tests, he carefully considered how he would explain the whole business, and although she didn't show up, he began to talk to her as if she were there, and to listen to her answers. In doing so, he understood much better what was consuming him, and once he distinctly imagined the old woman taking a little book out of her purse, an old notebook with a lot of crumbs stuck to it, probably cookies—she had opened it to look for a sentence that she had written down, and when she found it she brought her eyes close to the page, really close, and read it aloud.

"*Definitive resolutions are made always and only in a state of mind that is not destined to last.*"

"Who said that?"

"Marcel Proust. He was never wrong, that man."

And she closed the notebook.

Jasper Gwyn detested Proust, for reasons that he had never had the desire to examine, but he had saved that sentence years before, sure that someday or other it would be useful to him. Uttered by the voice of the old woman, it sounded incontrovertible. Then what should I do, he wondered.

"Be a copyist, for heaven's sake," answered the woman with the rain scarf.

"I'm not sure I know what it means."

"You'll understand. When it's right, you'll understand."

"Promise me."

"I promise."

Coming out of the stress test, the last day, Jasper Gwyn stopped at the reception desk and asked if they had seen a rather old woman who often came there to rest.

The young woman behind the window studied him a moment before answering.

"She passed away."

She used just that phrase.

"Several months ago," she added.

Jasper Gwyn stared at the young woman, bewildered.

"Did you know her?" she asked.

"Yes, we knew each other."

He turned instinctively to see if there was still an umbrella on the floor.

"But she didn't say anything to me," he said.

The young woman didn't ask questions, probably she intended to go back to her work.

"Maybe she didn't know," said Jasper Gwyn.

When he came out he spontaneously took the route he had taken with the old woman that day in the rain: because it was all he had of her.

Maybe he made a wrong turn, it was likely that he hadn't been very attentive that day, so he found himself on a street he didn't recognize, and the only thing that was the same was the rain, which had started suddenly, and was beating down hard. He looked for a café to take refuge in but there were none. Finally, trying to return to the clinic, he passed an art gallery. It was the sort of place where he never set foot, but then the rain made him inclined to seek shelter, and so he surprised himself by glancing in the window. There was a wooden floor, and the place seemed large and well lighted. Then Jasper Gwyn looked at the painting in the window. It was a portrait.

12.

They were large portraits, all similar, like the repetition of a single ambition, to infinity. There was always one person, nude, and almost nothing else, an empty room, a corridor. They were not handsome people, they were ordinary bodies. They were simply standing—but the force with which they did so was particular, as if they were geologic sediments, the result of millennial metamorphoses. Jasper Gwyn thought that they were stone, but soft, and living. He felt like touching them: he was convinced that they were *warm*.

At that point he would have left, that was enough, but outside it was still pouring, and so Jasper Gwyn, without realizing that this would mark his life, began to look through a catalogue of the show: there were three, open, on a light wood table, the usual large, ridiculously weighty books. Jasper Gwyn observed that the titles of the paintings were the rather stupid type you might expect (*Man with Hands on His Lap*), and that next to each title was written the date of execution. He noticed that the painter had worked on them for years, twenty, more or less, and yet, apparently, nothing in his way of seeing things, or in his technique, had changed. He had simply continued to paint—as if it were a single action, but very extended. Jasper Gwyn wondered if the same thing had been true for him, in the twelve years when he was writing, and while he was searching for an answer he came to the book's appendix, in which there were photographs taken while the painter was working, in his studio. Without realizing it he leaned over a little, to see better. He was struck by a photograph in which the painter was sitting placidly in a chair, turned toward the window, looking outside; nearby, a model whom Jasper Gwyn had just seen in one of the paintings on display in the gallery was lying nude on a couch, in a position not very different from the one in which she had been caught on the canvas. She, too, seemed to be gazing into emptiness.

Jasper Gwyn saw in it a time he hadn't expected, the passing of time. Like everyone, he imagined that that sort of thing happened in the usual way, with the painter at the easel and the model in place, motionless, the two engaged in a pas de deux whose rules they knew—he could imagine the foolish chatter, meanwhile. But here it was different, because painter and model seemed, rather, to be waiting, and one would have said that each was waiting on his own account—and for something that wasn't the painting. He thought that they were waiting to settle at the bottom of an enormous glass.

13.

He turned the page and the photographs were similar. The models changed, but the situation was almost always the same. One time the painter was washing his hands, another he was walking barefoot, looking down. He was never painting. A very tall, angular model, with big, childlike ears, was sitting on the edge of a bed, grasping the headboard with one hand. There was no reason to think that they were talking—that they had ever talked to each other.

Then Jasper Gwyn took the catalogue and looked for a place to sit. There were only two blue chairs, just in front of the table where a woman was working, amid papers and books. She must be the gallery manager, and Jasper Gwyn asked if he could sit there, or if it would bother her.

"Go ahead," said the woman.

She was wearing bizarre reading glasses and when she touched things she did it with the caution of a woman who has manicured nails.

Jasper Gwyn sat down, and although he was at a distance from the woman that made sense only in the light of a mutual desire to exchange a few words, he set the book on his lap and began looking again at those photographs as if he were alone, at home.

The painter's studio seemed empty and rundown, without a trace of conscious cleanliness, yet you had the impression of an unreal disorder, since there was nothing that could, if necessary, be put in order. Analogously, the nudity of the models seemed to be the result not of an absence of clothes but of a sort of original condition, existing before any modesty—or much later. One of the photographs showed a man of about sixty, with a carefully trimmed mustache, and white hair on his chest, who was sitting on a chair, drinking from a cup, maybe tea, his legs slightly spread, his feet placed slightly on edge on the cold floor. You would have said that he was absolutely unfit for nakedness, to the point of avoiding it even in domestic or erotic intimacy, but there he was, in fact, perfectly naked, his penis lying sideways, rather large, and circumcised, and although it was undoubtedly grotesque it was also, at the same time, so *inevitable* that for a moment Jasper Gwyn was sure that man knew something that he didn't.

Then he raised his head, looked around, and immediately found the portrait of the man with the mustache, a big one, hanging on the wall opposite: it was him, without the cup of tea, but in the same chair, naked, his feet placed slightly on edge on the cold floor. He seemed enormous, but above all he seemed to have *arrived*.

"Do you like it?" the gallery manager asked.

Jasper Gwyn was understanding something particular, which was to change the course of his days, and so he didn't answer right away. He looked again at the photograph in the catalogue, then again at the painting on the wall—it was evident that something had happened, between the photo and the painting, something like a *journey*. Jasper Gwyn thought that it must have taken a lot of time, some sort of exile, and certainly the overcoming of many resistances. He didn't have in mind any technical trick, nor did the skill of the painter seem important; only it occurred to him that patience had set a goal, and in the end what it had achieved was to *take home* the man with the mustache. It seemed to him a very beautiful act.

14.

He turned to the gallery manager, he owed her an answer.

"No," he said. "I *never* like paintings."

"Ah," said the gallery manager.

She smiled, understanding, as if a child had said that when he grew up he wanted to be a window washer.

"And what don't you like about paintings?" she asked patiently.

Again Jasper Gwyn didn't answer. He was thinking of that idea of leading someone back home. It had never occurred to him that a portrait could *take someone home*; in fact, he had always found just the opposite—it was evident that portraits were made to display a false identity and pass it off as true. Who would ever pay to be unmasked by a painter, to hang on a wall of your house the part of yourself you labored to hide every day?

Who would ever pay? he repeated slowly to himself.

He looked up at the gallery manager.

"Excuse me, do you have a piece of paper and something to write with, please?"

The gallery manager handed him a notepad and a pencil.

Jasper Gwyn wrote something, a few lines. Then he looked at them for a long time. He seemed absorbed in a thought so fragile that the gallery manager remained motionless, as when one doesn't want to cause a sparrow to fly off the railing. Jasper Gwyn said something in a low voice, but something indecipherable. Finally he took the sheet of paper, folded it in four, and put it in his pocket. He looked up again at the gallery manager.

"They're mute," he said.

"I'm sorry?"

"I don't like paintings because they're mute. They're like people who move their lips to speak, but you don't hear their voice. You have to imagine it. I don't like to make that effort."

Then he got up and went to stand in front of the portrait of the man with the mustache, and for a long time, again, remained absorbed in his thoughts—a very long time.

He went home heedless of the rain that was still beating down, and cold. Every so often he said something out loud. He was talking to the woman with the rain scarf.

15.

"Portraits?"

"Yes, why?"

Tom Bruce Shepperd considered his words carefully.

"Jasper, you don't know how to draw."

"Right. The idea is to write them."

A couple of weeks after that morning at the gallery, Jasper Gwyn had telephoned Tom to tell him that there was a new development. He also wanted to tell him to stop sending him contracts to sign which he never even opened. But mainly he telephoned about the new development.

He had to tell him that, after searching at length for a new job, he had now found it. Tom didn't take it well.

"You *have* a job. You write books."

"I stopped, Tom, how often do I have to tell you?"

"No one is aware of it."

"What do you mean?"

"That you can start again tomorrow."

"I'm sorry, but even if I had, absurdly, decided to start writing again, what a nerve I'd have, don't you think, after what I wrote in the *Guardian*?"

"The list? Brilliant provocation. Avant-garde act. And then who's going to remember?"

Tom wasn't only his agent, he was the man who had discovered him, twelve years earlier. They went to the same pub, at the time, and once they had stayed till closing talking about what Hemingway would have written if he hadn't shot himself with a hunting rifle at the age of sixty-two.

"Not a goddamn thing," Tom had maintained. But Jasper Gwyn had a different opinion, and finally Tom had guessed, in spite of four dark beers, that this man understood literature, and had asked him what he did. Jasper Gwyn had told him and Tom had made him repeat it, because he really couldn't believe it.

"I would have said professor, or journalist, something like that."

"No, nothing of the sort."

"Well, it's a pity."

"Why?"

"I don't have the slightest idea, I'm drunk. You know what I do?"

"No."

"Literary agent."

He had taken out a business card and handed it to Jasper Gwyn.

"If by chance someday you happen to write something, don't do me the injustice of forgetting me. You know, it happens to everyone, sooner or later."

"What?"

"Writing something."

He had an instant of reflection.

"Also forgetting me, naturally."

They hadn't talked about it again, and when they met at the pub they sat together gladly, often talking about books and writers. But one day Tom opened an enormous yellow envelope that had arrived in the morning mail, and inside was Jasper Gwyn's novel. He had opened it at random, and had begun to read at that point. There was a school that was on fire. It had all started there.

Now, however, everything seemed to be ending, and Tom Bruce Shepperd didn't even understand why. The list of fifty-two things, all right, but it couldn't be only that. All true writers hate the trappings of the profession, but no one stops for that reason. Usually one more drink is enough, or a young wife with a certain propensity for spending money. Unfortunately Jasper Gwyn drank one glass of whiskey a day, always at the same time, as if he were oiling a clock. Furthermore, he didn't believe in marriage. So it seemed there was nothing to be done. Now he had also added this business of the portraits.

"It's a very private thing, Tom, swear you won't discuss it with anyone."

"You can count on that, since who do you think would believe me?"

When Tom married Lottie, a Hungarian woman twenty-three years younger than he was, Jasper Gwyn had been the witness, and at a certain point during the dinner had stood up on a table and recited a Shakespeare sonnet. Only it wasn't by Shakespeare, it was his, a perfect imitation. The last two lines were: *If I have to forget you I will remember to do so, but then don't ask me to forget that I remembered.* Then Tom had hugged him, not so much for the sonnet, which he hadn't really understood, but because he knew what it must have cost him to climb up on a table and get people's attention. He had really hugged him. Now, for the same reason, he couldn't take the business of the portraits well.

"Try to explain it to me," he asked.

"I don't know, I thought I'd like to make portraits."

"Okay, that I understand."

"Naturally I'm not talking about paintings. I'd like to *write* portraits."

"Yes."

"But all the rest would be the way it is with portraits…the studio, the model, it would all be the same."

"You'd pose them?"

"Something like that."

"And then?"

"Then I imagine it would take a lot of time. But at the end I'll start writing, and what comes out of it will be a portrait."

"A portrait in what sense? A description?"

Jasper Gwyn had thought about it for a long time. In fact that was the problem.

"No, a description, no, that wouldn't make sense."

"That's what painters do. There's the arm, and the painter paints it, that's it. And what would you do? You'd write things like 'the white arm lies softly' etcetera, etcetera?"

"No, exactly, that's not even thinkable."

"And so?"

"I don't know."

"You don't know?"

"No. I'd have to put myself in the situation where I'm making a portrait and then I could discover what it means, exactly, to write instead of paint. To write a portrait."

"That is, at this moment you don't have the slightest idea."

"Something, some hypotheses."

"Like?"

"I don't know, I imagine it would be a matter of *taking people home*."

"Taking them home?"

"I don't know, I don't think I can explain it to you."

"I need a drink. Stay on the line, don't even think of hanging up."

Jasper Gwyn kept hold of the receiver. He heard Tom muttering in the background. Then he put down the receiver and walked slowly toward the bathroom, while a lot of ideas whirled around in his head, all having to do with the portraits. He thought that the only thing to do was to try it, and, besides, he certainly hadn't known where he wanted to end up when he started the thriller about the disappearances in Wales—he had just had in mind a certain way of proceeding. He peed. And then, too, if Tom had made him explain before he started to write what he intended to do, likely he wouldn't have known what to say. He flushed. It makes no more sense to start a novel, the first, than to rent a studio to make portraits without knowing exactly what it means. He went back to the telephone and picked up the receiver.

"Tom?"

"Jasper, can I be sincere?"

"Of course."

"As a book it will be colossal nonsense."

"No, you don't understand, it won't be a book."

"What, then?"

Jasper Gwyn had imagined that people would take home the pages he had written, and would keep them shut up in a drawer, or put them on a low table. As you might keep a photograph, or hang a painting on the wall. This was an aspect of the matter that excited him. No more fifty-two things, just an agreement between him and those people. It was like making a table for them, or washing their car. A job. He would write what they were, that's all. He would be, for them, a copyist.

"They'll just be portraits," he said. "The people who pay to have them done will take them home and the thing ends there."

"Pay?"

"Of course, people pay, no? To have a portrait done."

"Jasper, those are paintings, and, anyway, people long ago

stopped having their portraits done, except for the Queen and a couple of feeble-minded types who have walls to fill."

"Yes, but mine are written, it's different."

"It's worse!"

"I don't know."

They were silent for a moment. He heard Tom swallowing his whiskey.

"Jasper, maybe it's better if we talk about it another time."

"Yes, probably, yes."

"Let's sleep on it and then talk again."

"Okay."

"I have to metabolize it."

"Yes, I understand."

"Otherwise everything's fine?"

"Yes."

"Do you need anything?"

"No. That is, one thing, maybe."

"Tell me."

"Do you know a real-estate broker?"

"Someone who looks for houses?"

"Yes."

"John Septimus Hill, he's the best. You remember him?"

Jasper Gwyn seemed to remember a very tall man, with impeccable manners, dressed with meticulous elegance. He was at the wedding.

"Go to him, he's perfect," said Tom.

"Thanks."

"What is it, are you moving?"

"No, I thought of renting a studio, a place for attempting that portrait."

Tom Bruce Shepperd rolled his eyes.

16.

When John Septimus Hill handed him the form to fill out, in which the client was asked to specify his requirements, Jasper Gwyn tried to read the questions, but finally he looked up from the papers and asked if he could tell him.

"I'm sure I'd manage to explain better."

John Septimus Hill took the form, looked at it skeptically, then threw it in the wastebasket.

"I've never yet met anyone who had the kindness to fill it out."

Then he explained that it had been an idea of his son's. His son had been working with him for several months; he was twenty-seven, and had decided to modernize the style of the firm.

"I tend to believe that the old way of doing things worked very well," continued John Septimus Hill, "but you can imagine how one always behaves with a sort of mad indulgence toward one's children. Do you have children, by any chance?"

"No," said Jasper Gwyn. "I don't believe in marriage and I'm not fit to have children."

"Very reasonable position. Would you begin by telling me how many square feet you need?"

Jasper Gwyn was prepared and gave a precise answer.

"I need a single room half as big as a tennis court."

John Septimus Hill didn't turn a hair.

"On what floor?" he asked.

Jasper Gwyn explained that he imagined it facing on an interior garden, but he added that maybe also a top floor would work, the important thing was that it should be absolutely silent and peaceful. He would like it to have, he concluded, an uncared-for floor.

John Septimus Hill didn't take any notes, but seemed to be piling up in some corner of his mind all the information, as if it were ironed sheets.

They talked about heating, bathrooms, doorman, kitchen, trim, fixtures, and parking. On every subject Jasper Gwyn demonstrated that he had clear ideas. He was categorical in stating that the space had to be empty, in fact very empty. The mere term *furnished* annoyed him. He tried to explain, and succeeded, that he wouldn't mind some water stains, here and there, and maybe some pipes, preferably in a state of disrepair. He insisted on blinds and shutters on the windows, so that he could regulate the light in the room as he wished. Traces of old wallpaper on the walls he wouldn't mind. The doors, if they were really necessary, should be of wood, possibly a bit swollen. A high ceiling, he decreed.

John Septimus Hill piled up everything carefully, his eyes halfclosed, as if he had just finished a heavy lunch, then he was silent for a bit, apparently satisfied. Finally he reopened his eyes and cleared his throat.

"May I be permitted a question that could legitimately be called reasonably private?"

Jasper Gwyn didn't say yes or no. John Septimus Hill took it as encouragement.

"You have a job that requires an absurdly high degree of precision and perfectionism, right?"

Jasper Gwyn, without really understanding why, thought of divers. Then he answered that yes, in the past, he had done a job of that sort.

"May I ask you what it was? It's simply curiosity, believe me."

Jasper Gwyn said that for a while he had written books.

John Septimus Hill weighed the answer, as if he were waiting to find out if he could understand it without greatly disturbing his own convictions.

17.

Ten days later, John Septimus Hill took Jasper Gwyn to a low factory building, at the back of a garden, behind Marylebone High Street. For years it had been a carpenter's storeroom. Then, in rapid succession, it had been the warehouse for an art gallery, the offices of a travel magazine, and the garage of a collector of vintage motorcycles. Jasper Gwyn found it perfect. He much appreciated the indelible oil stains left by the motorcycles on the wooden floor and the edges of posters showing Caribbean seas that no one had troubled to take off the walls. There was a small bathroom on the roof, reached by an iron stairway. There was no trace of a kitchen. The big windows could be blocked by massive wooden shutters, just redone and not yet painted. One entered the big room by a double door that opened onto the garden. There were also pipes visible, which were not in good shape. John Septimus Hill noted, in a professional tone, that for the water stains it wouldn't be hard to find a solution.

"Although it's the first time," he observed without irony, "that dampness has been mentioned to me as a hoped-for decoration, rather than a disaster."

They settled on a price, and Jasper Gwyn agreed to it for six months, reserving the right to renew the contract for six more. The figure was substantial, and this helped him realize that if it had ever been a game, that business of the portraits, it was so no longer.

"Good, my son will take care of the practical details," said John Septimus Hill as they parted. They were on the street, in front of a tube station. "Don't take this as a polite observation," he added, "but it's been a real pleasure to do business with you."

Jasper Gwyn wasn't good at farewells, even in their lightest form, like a goodbye from a real-estate broker who had just found him a former garage in which to attempt to write portraits. But he also felt a sincere liking for this man, and he wanted to be able to express it. So, instead of saying something generically nice, he murmured something that amazed even him.

"I didn't always write books," he said. "Before that I had another profession. I did it for nine years."

"Really?"

"I was a tuner. I tuned pianos. The same profession as my father."

John Septimus Hill took in the information with evident satisfaction.

"There. Now I think I understand better. Thank you."

Then he said there was something he had always wondered about tuners.

"I've always wondered if they know how to play the piano. Professionally, I mean."

"Seldom," answered Jasper Gwyn. "And yet," he continued, "if the question you have in mind is how in the world, after working for hours, they refrain from sitting down right there to play a polonaise by Chopin, so as to enjoy the result of their dedication and knowledge, the answer is that, even if they were able to, they never would."

"No?"

"A man who tunes a piano doesn't like to untune it," Jasper Gwyn explained.

They parted, promising to meet again.

Days later, Jasper Gwyn was sitting on the floor in a corner of a former garage that was now his portrait studio. He turned the key over in his hands, and examined the distances, the light, the details. There was a great silence, broken only by the sporadic gurgling of the water pipes. He sat there for a long time, analyzing his next moves. He would have to put something there—a bed, maybe, some chairs. He thought of how to light it, and where he would be. He tried to imagine himself there, in the silent company of a stranger, both of them surrendered to a time about which they would have to learn everything. He already felt the grip of an uncontrollable embarrassment.

"I'll never do it," he said at one point.

"Come on," said the lady with the rain scarf. "Have a whiskey if you've really got cold feet."

"It wouldn't be enough."

"Double whiskey, then."

"You make it seem easy."

"What's the matter, are you afraid?"

"Yes."

"Good. If there's no fear you can't accomplish anything good. And the water stains?"

"It seems that I just have to wait. The heating pipes are disgusting."

"You're reassuring me."

The next day Jasper Gwyn decided to think about the music. All that silence made an impression, and he had reached the conclusion that he had to give the room a lining of sound. The gurgling of the pipes was fine, but it was obvious that he could do better.

18.

He had known many composers, in the years when he tuned pianos, but the one who came to mind was David Barber. It was logical: Jasper Gwyn distinctly recalled a composition of his for clarinet, fan, and plumbing pipes. It wasn't even so bad. The pipes gurgled a lot.

For years they had been out of touch, but when Jasper Gwyn gained a certain fame David Barber had sought him out to propose that he write the text for a cantata. He hadn't done anything about it (it was a cantata for recorded voice, seltzer siphon, and string orchestra), but the two had remained in contact. David was a likable fellow, his hobby was hunting, and he lived in the midst of dogs, all of whom were named for pianists, something that allowed Jasper Gwyn to declare, without lying, that he had once been bitten by Radu Lupu. As a composer David had for a long time enjoyed hanging out with the more festive wing of the New York avant-garde: he didn't make much money, but success with women was assured. Then for a long period he had disappeared, following certain esoteric ideas he had about tonal relationships and teaching what he apparently had learned in various university-type circles. The last Jasper Gwyn had heard of him was when, in the papers, he had read about a symphony performed, unconventionally, at Old Trafford, the famous stadium in Manchester. The title of the work, ninety minutes long, was *Semifinal.*

Without too much effort he found the address, and appeared one morning at his house, in Fulham. When David Barber opened the door and saw him, he gave him a big hug, as if he had been expecting him. Then they went to the park together, to take Martha Argerich to shit. He was a spinone from the Vendée.

19.

There was no need to beat around the bush with David, and so Jasper Gwyn said simply that he needed something to use as a soundtrack for his new studio. He said he wasn't capable of working in silence.

"You never thought of some good records?" David Barber asked.

"That's music. I want sounds."

"Sounds or noises?"

"You didn't use to think there was a difference."

They went on talking, walking in the park, while Martha

Argerich chased squirrels. Jasper Gwyn said that what he imagined was a very long, barely perceptible loop that would just cover the silence, muffling it.

"How long is very long?" asked David Barber.

"I don't know. Fifty hours?"

David Barber stopped. He laughed.

"Well, it's no joke. It will cost you a certain amount, my friend."

Then he said that he wanted to see the place. And think about it a little, while sitting there. So they decided to go together to the studio behind Marylebone High Street the next morning. They spent the rest of the time recalling days gone by, and at one point David Barber said that for a while, years earlier, he'd been certain that Jasper had gone to bed with his girlfriend. She was some sort of Swedish photographer. No, it's she who went to bed with me, said Jasper Gwyn, I didn't understand a thing. They laughed about it.

The next day David Barber arrived in a broken-down station wagon that smelled of wet dog even from a distance. He parked in front of a hydrant, because it was his personal way of protesting the government's management of cultural funds. They went into the studio and closed the door behind them. There was a great silence, apart from the gurgling pipes, naturally.

"Nice," said David Barber.

"Yes."

"You should pay attention to those water stains."

"It's all under control."

David Barber wandered around the room for a while, and took the measure of that particular silence. He listened attentively to the pipes, and assessed the squeaking of the wooden floor.

"Maybe I should also know what type of book you're writing," he said.

Jasper Gwyn had a moment of discomfort. He wasn't yet used to the idea that it would take a lifetime to convince the world that he was no longer writing. It was an astonishing phenomenon. Once an editor he met on the street had complimented him warmly on his article in the *Guardian*. Immediately afterward he had asked, "What are you writing now?" These were things that Jasper Gwyn wasn't able to understand.

"Believe me, what I'm writing isn't important," he said.

And he explained that what he wanted was a background of sound that would change like light during the day, and thus imperceptibly and continuously. Above all: elegant. This was very important. He added that he wanted something in which there was no trace of rhythm, but only a becoming that would suspend time, and simply fill the space with a journey that had no coordinates. He said he would like something as motionless as a face that is aging.

"Where's the bathroom?" David Barber asked.

When he returned he said that he accepted.

"Ten thousand pounds plus the sound system. Let's say twenty thousand pounds."

Jasper Gwyn liked the thought that he was using up all his savings gambling on a profession whose existence he wasn't even sure of. He wanted somehow to put his back to the wall, because he knew that only then would he have a chance to find, in himself, what he was seeking. So he agreed.

A month later David Barber came to install the sound system and then he left Jasper Gwyn a hard disk.

"Enjoy it. It's seventy-two hours, it came out a little long. I couldn't find the ending."

That night Jasper Gwyn lay down on the floor, in his copyist's studio, and started the loop. It began with what seemed a sound of leaves and continued on, moving imperceptibly, and coming upon sounds of every type as if by chance. Tears came to Jasper Gwyn's eyes.

20.

During the month while he was waiting for David Barber's music, or whatever it was, Jasper Gwyn had been busy refining other details. He had begun with the furniture. In the warehouse of a junk shop on Regent Street he had found three chairs and an iron bed, rather beat-up, but with a certain style. He had added two shabby leather armchairs the color of cricket balls. He rented two enormous and expensive carpets and bought at an unreasonable price a wall coatrack that came from a French brasserie. At one point he was tempted by a horse from an eighteenth-century merry-go-round and then he realized that things were getting out of hand.

One thing he couldn't immediately focus on was how he would write, whether standing or sitting at a desk, on a computer, by hand, on big sheets of paper, or in small notebooks. He still had to find out if in fact he was going to write, or if he would confine himself to observing and thinking, then, later, maybe at home, assembling what had occurred to him. For painters it was simple, they had the canvas in front of them—that wasn't strange. But someone who wished, instead, to write? He could hardly be sitting at a table, in front of a computer. He finally realized that anything would be ridiculous except to start work and discover on the spot, at the right moment, what it made sense to do and what it didn't. So no desk, no laptop, not even a pencil the first day, he decided. He allowed himself only a modest shoe rack, to place in a corner: he imagined that he would like, each time, to be able to put on the shoes that that day seemed to him most fitting.

Occupied by all these things, he had immediately felt better, and for a while he no longer had to keep at bay the crises that had afflicted him for months. When he felt the sensation of disappearing, whose arrival he had come to recognize, he refused to get frightened and concentrated on his thousands of tasks, carrying them out with an even more maniacal scrupulousness. In attention to the details he found instant relief. This led him, at times, to reach almost literary peaks of perfectionism. He happened, for example, to find himself in the presence of an artisan who made light bulbs. Not lamps: bulbs. He made them by hand. He was an old man with a gloomy workshop in the neighborhood of Camden Town. Jasper Gwyn had looked for him for a long time without even knowing whether he existed, and had finally found him. What he intended to ask him for was not only a very particular light—*childish*, he would explain— but, in particular, a light that would last for a certain predetermined time. He wanted bulbs that would go out after thirty-two days.

"All at once or suffering death throes?" asked the old man, as if he were thoroughly acquainted with the problem.

21.

The matter of the light bulbs may seem of dubious relevance, but for Jasper Gwyn it had, instead, become a crucial issue. It had to do with time. Although he still hadn't the least idea of what the act of *writing a portrait* could be, he had come up with a certain idea of its possible duration—as it is possible to decipher the distance and not the identity of a man walking at night. He had immediately dismissed something rapid, but it was also hard to imagine an action whose ending was random and possibly very far off. So he had begun to measure—lying on the floor, in the studio, in absolute solitude—the weight of the hours and the texture of the days. He had in mind a journey, similar to what he had seen in the paintings that day, and he intended to work out the pace at which it could be made, and the length of the road that would bring it to a destination. He had to identify the speed at which embarrassments would dissolve and the slowness with which some truth would rise to the surface. He realized that, as in life, only a certain punctuality could make that act complete—as it makes some moments of the living happy.

In the end he had decided that thirty-two days might represent a first, credible approximation. He determined that he would try one work session a day, for thirty-two days, four hours a day. And here was the importance of the light bulbs.

The fact is that he couldn't imagine something that stopped abruptly, at the end of the last sitting, in a bureaucratic and impersonal way. It was obvious that the end of the work would have to be an elegant process, perhaps poetic, and possibly unpredictable. Then he found the solution he had been working on for the light—eighteen bulbs hanging from the ceiling, at regular intervals, in a perfect geometry—and he imagined that around the thirty-second day those bulbs would begin to go out one by one, randomly, but all in an interval of time that was no less than two days and no more than a week. He saw the studio glide into darkness, in patches, following an arbitrary pattern, and he fantasized about how they would move around, he and the model, in order to make use of the last lights, or, on the contrary, to take refuge in the first dark places. He saw himself distinctly in the weak light of a last bulb giving belated touches to the portrait. And then accepting the darkness, at the dying of the last filament.

It's perfect, he thought.

That was why he found himself in the presence of the old man, in Camden Town.

"No, they should just die, without agonizing, and without any noise, if possible."

The old man made one of those indecipherable gestures that artisans make to revenge themselves on the world. Then he explained that light bulbs were not easy creatures, they were affected by a lot of variables and often had their own, unpredictable form of madness.

"Usually," he added, "the client at this point says, 'Like women.' Spare me, please."

"Like children," said Jasper Gwyn.

The old man nodded in agreement. Like all artisans he spoke only as he worked, and in his case this meant holding in his fingers some small bulbs, as if they were eggs, and immersing them in an opaque solution that looked vaguely like a distillate. The purpose of the operation was openly inscrutable. Then he dried them with a hair dryer as old as he was.

They wasted a lot of time digressing on the nature of light bulbs, and Jasper Gwyn ended up discovering a universe whose existence he had never even suspected. He particularly liked learning that the shapes of light bulbs are infinite, but there are sixteen principal ones, and for each there is a name. In an elegant convention, they are all names of queens or princesses. Jasper Gwyn chose the Catherine de Médicis, because it looked like a teardrop that had escaped from a chandelier.

"Thirty-two days?" the old man asked when he decided that this man deserved his work.

"That's the idea."

"I'd have to know how many times you turn them off and on."

"Once," Jasper Gwyn answered, impeccable.

"How do you know?"

"I know."

The old man stopped and looked up at Jasper Gwyn. He stared at him, so to speak, in the filament of his eyes. He looked for something that he couldn't find. A crack. Then he lowered his gaze back to his work and his hands started up again.

"It will take a lot of care to transport them and mount them," he said. "Do you know how to hold a bulb in your hand?"

"I've never wondered," Jasper Gwyn answered.

The old man handed him one. It was an Elizabeth Romanov. Jasper Gwyn held it cautiously in the palm of his hand. The old man grimaced.

"Use your fingers. Like that you'll kill it."

Jasper Gwyn obeyed.

"Bayonet joint," the old man stated, shaking his head. "If I give you the ones with screws you might do me in before they're lighted." He took back his Elizabeth Romanov.

They agreed that nine days later the old man would deliver to Jasper Gwyn eighteen Catherine de Médicis destined to go out in an arc of time that would vary between 760 hours and 830 hours. They would go out without gasping, in vain flashes, silently. They would do so one by one, in an order that no one could predict.

"We forgot to talk about the type of light," said Jasper Gwyn as he was about to leave.

"What do you want?"

"Childlike."

"All right." They shook hands goodbye, and Jasper Gwyn realized that he had done so cautiously, just as, many years earlier, he had been accustomed to do with pianists.

22.

Nice, said the woman in the rain scarf. She began to dry her umbrella on a radiator, and walked around examining the details from close up. The shoe rack, the warm colors of the carpets, the stains of dampness on the walls, of oil on the floor. She made sure that the bed was not too soft, and tried the armchairs. Nice, she said.

Standing in a corner of his new studio, his coat still on, Jasper Gwyn looked at what he had assembled in a month and a half, out of nothing, pursuing a foolish idea. He found no mistakes, and thought that everything had been done with attention and balance, in the same way a copyist could have arranged paper and pen on the table, put on the cloth oversleeves, chosen the ink, sure of recognizing the most appropriate shade of blue. He thought that he wasn't wrong: it was a magnificent profession. For a moment the idea of a rusting iron nameplate on the door crossed his mind. JASPER GWYN. COPYIST.

"It's surprising how pointless it all is in the absence of a model," observed the woman in the rain scarf. "Or did I not see it?" she added, looking around with the air of one who is looking for the sauce aisle in the supermarket.

"No, no model, for now," said Jasper Gwyn.

"I imagine there's not exactly a line out the door."

"Not yet."

"Do you have an idea of how to resolve it, or are you going to put it off until the lease expires?"

Every so often the old woman's tones reverted to those of a schoolmistress. That gruff way of caring about something.

"No, I have a plan," answered Jasper Gwyn.

"Let's hear it."

Jasper Gwyn had thought about it at length. It was evident that he would have to hire someone, the first time, to test himself. But he would have to choose carefully, because a model who was too difficult would discourage him pointlessly, and one too easy wouldn't push him to find what he was looking for. Nor was it easy to imagine what might be the right degree of acquaintance for that first experiment. A friend, so to speak, would make the job much easier, but would falsify the experiment, because he would already know too many things about him, and it wouldn't be possible to look at him as at an unfamiliar landscape. On the other hand, to choose a perfect stranger, as logic would suggest, implied a whole series of embarrassments that Jasper Gwyn would prefer to spare himself, at least that first time. Apart from the difficulty of explaining the thing, of understanding the type of work they were to do together, there was that question of nudity—awkward. Instinctively, Jasper Gwyn felt that nudity was an indisputable condition. He imagined it as a kind of necessary goad. It would move everything beyond a certain limit, and without that uncomfortable dislocation he felt that no field would open up, no infinite prospect. So he had to resign himself. The model had to be nude. But Jasper Gwyn was a reserved man, and appreciated shyness. He had no familiarity with bodies and in his life had worked only with sounds and thoughts. The mechanism of a piano was the most physical thing he had had the opportunity to master. If he thought of a nude model, before him, what he felt was only a profound embarrassment and an inevitable bewilderment. So the choice of the first model was delicate, and the idea of choosing a perfect stranger imprudent.

Finally, just to simplify things somewhat, Jasper Gwyn had decided to exclude the idea of a man. He couldn't do it. It was a matter not of homophobia but of simply being unused to it. There was no need to complicate life too much, in that first experiment: to learn to look at a male body was something that, for the moment, he preferred to put off. A woman would definitely be better, he wouldn't be starting from zero. The choice of a woman, however, had implications that Jasper Gwyn was perfectly aware of. He added the variable of desire. He would like to start with a body that would be beautiful to discover, look at, spy on. But it was clear that making a portrait was an act that had to be sheltered from pure and simple desire, or that, at most, might start off from desire and then would let it, in some way, wane. Making a portrait had to be a matter of distant intimacies. And so too much beauty would have been out of place. Too little, on the other hand, would be a pointless affliction. What Jasper Gwyn sought was a woman who would be beautiful to look at but not so beautiful that he would end up wanting her.

"Let's get to the point, did you find her?" asked the woman in the rain scarf as she unwrapped a citrus-flavored candy.

"Yes, I think so."

"And so?"

"I have to find a way of asking her. It's not that easy."

"It's a job, Mr. Gwyn, you're not asking her to go to bed."

"I know, but it's a strange job."

"If you explain it to her, she'll understand. And if she doesn't understand, a generous compensation will help her clarify her ideas. Because you've provided for a generous compensation, right?"

"I don't exactly know."

"What's the matter, you're becoming a skinflint?"

"No, it's not that, come on, it's that I don't want to offend. Ultimately, it's money in exchange for a naked body."

"Of course, if you put it like that…"

"It *is* like that."

"Not true. Only a puritan full of complexes like you could imagine describing the thing in those terms."

"Do you have a better idea?"

"Of course."

"Let's hear it."

"'Miss, in exchange for five thousand pounds, would you allow me to look at you for around thirty days, just the time to transcribe your secret?' It's not a sentence that's difficult to utter. Practice in front of the mirror, it helps."

"Five thousand is a lot."

"What are you doing, starting that again?"

Jasper Gwyn looked at her, smiling, and loved her dearly. For a moment he thought that it would have been simple with her, it would have been a perfect way to begin, with that woman.

"Forget it, I'm too old. You shouldn't start with an old person, too difficult."

"You're not old. You're dead."

The woman shrugged. "Dying is only a particularly exact way of getting old."

When he got home, Jasper Gwyn practiced a little in front of the mirror. Then he telephoned Tom Bruce Shepperd. It was two in the morning.

23.

"Shit, Jasper, it's 2 a.m. I'm in bed!"

"Were you sleeping?"

"Sleeping isn't the only thing you can do in a bed."

"Ah."

"Lottie says hello."

In the background he heard Lottie's voice that, with no rancor, was saying Hi, Jasper. She was good-natured.

"I'm sorry, Tom."

"Forget it. What is it, are you lost again? Should I send Rebecca to get you?"

"No, no, I'm not lost anymore. But, in fact... to tell you the truth, I wanted to talk to you about her."

"About Rebecca?"

What Jasper Gwyn thought was that that girl was perfect. He had in mind how the unquestionable beauty of her face provoked a desire that her body then denied, with its slow, placid manner: perfect. She was poison and antidote—in a sweet and enigmatic way. Jasper Gwyn hadn't met her a single time without feeling a childlike desire to touch her, just slightly: but as he would have liked to put his fingers on a shiny insect, or a steamed-up window. In addition, he knew her, but he didn't know her; she seemed to be at the right distance, in that intermediate zone where any further intimacy would have been a slow but not impossible conquest. He knew that he could look at her for a long time without feeling uneasy, without desire, and without ever getting bored.

"Rebecca, yes, the intern."

Tom burst out laughing.

"Hey, Jasper, we've got a weakness for fat girls?"

He turned to Lottie.

"Listen to this, Jasper likes Rebecca."

In the background he heard Lottie's sleepy voice saying Rebecca who?

"Jasper, big brother, you never stop surprising me."

"Will you cut out the vulgar remarks and listen to me?"

"Okay."

"It's serious."

"You're in love?"

"It's serious in the sense that it's about work."

Tom put on his glasses. Under the circumstances it was his way of opening the office.

"She persuaded you to do scenes from books that you'll never write? I told you she was a smart girl."

"No, Tom, it's not about that. I need her for my work. But not that."

"Take her. Provided you go back to writing, it's fine with me."

"It's not so simple."

"Why?"

"I want to make her my first portrait. You know, the thing about the portraits?"

Tom remembered it very well. "I'm not mad about that idea, you know, Jasper."

"I know, but now it's a different problem. I need Rebecca to come to my studio to pose for around thirty days. I'll pay her. But she'll tell me she doesn't want to lose her job with you."

"To *pose*?"

"I want to try it."

"You're crazy."

"Maybe. But now I need that favor. Let her work for me for a month or so, and then you'll take her back."

They went on talking for a while, and it was a wonderful phone call, because they ended up discussing the profession of writing and things they both loved. Jasper Gwyn explained that the circumstances of the portrait appealed to him because they compelled him to force his talent into an uncomfortable position. He realized that the premises were ridiculous, but that was precisely what appealed to him, in the suspicion that if you removed from writing the natural possibility of the novel, it would do something to survive, a movement, something. He also said that the something would be what people would then buy and take home. He added that it would be the unpredictable product of a domestic and private rite, not intended to return to the surface of the world, and thus removed from the sufferings that afflicted the profession of writer. In fact, he concluded, we're talking about a different profession. A possible name was: copyist.

Tom listened. He tried to understand.

"I don't see how you will be able to get around the white arm resting softly on the hip or the gaze as luminous as an eastern dawn," he said at one point. "And for that kind of thing, hard to imagine doing better than a Dickens or a Hardy."

"Yes, of course, if I stop there defeat is certain."

"You're sure there's something beyond?"

"Sure, no. I have to try, I told you."

"Then let's say this: I hand over my intern and don't get in your way, but you promise me that if at the end of the experiment you really haven't found something, you'll go back to writing. Books, I mean."

"What's that, blackmail?"

"A pact. If you don't succeed, you'll do as I say. Start with the scenes from books you'll never write, or whatever you want. But you give the studio back to John Septimus Hill and sign a nice new contract."

"I could find someone else to come and pose."

"But you want Rebecca."

"Yes."

"So?"

Jasper Gwyn thought that all in all he didn't mind the little game. The idea that failure would take him back to the horror of the fifty-two things he never wanted to do again suddenly seemed to him galvanizing. In the end he agreed. It was almost three in the morning, and he agreed. Tom thought he was about to recover one of the few writers he represented whom he could truly consider a friend.

"Tomorrow I'll send you Rebecca. In the Laundromat, as usual?"

"Maybe a somewhat quieter place would be better."

"The bar of the Stafford Hotel, then. At five?"

"All right."

"Don't stand her up."

"No."

"Did I already tell you I love you?"

"Not tonight."

"Strange."

They spent another ten minutes talking nonsense. A couple of sixteen-year-olds.

24.

The next day, at five, Jasper Gwyn appeared at the Stafford Hotel, but only out of courtesy, because in the meantime he had decided to forget about it, having reached the conclusion that the idea of talking to that girl was completely outside his ability. Still, when Rebecca arrived, he chose a quiet table, right against a window that looked onto the street, and the first remarks—about the weather and the traffic that at that hour made everything impossible—weren't difficult. Eager to order a whiskey, he ordered an apple juice with ice instead and remembered some little pastries they did very well there. "For me, coffee," said Rebecca. Like all truly fat people, she didn't touch pastries. She was radiant, in her aimless beauty.

First they talked about things that had nothing to do with it, just to take the measure of things, as one does. Rebecca said that elegant hotels intimidated her somewhat, but Jasper Gwyn pointed out how there are few things in the world as nice as hotel lobbies.

"The people who come and go," he said. "And all those secrets."

Then he let out a confession, something he didn't usually do, and said that in another life he would like to be a hotel lobby.

"You mean *work* in a lobby?"

"No, no, *be* a lobby, physically. Even in a three-star hotel, it doesn't matter."

Then Rebecca laughed, and when Jasper Gwyn asked her what she thought she'd like to be in the next life, she said, "An anorexic rock star," and she seemed to have had the answer ready forever.

So after a while everything was simpler, and Jasper Gwyn thought he could try it, say what he had in mind. He took a slightly roundabout route, but that was, in any case, his way of doing things.

"May I ask if you trust me, Rebecca? I mean, are you sure that you're sitting across from a well-brought-up person who would never put you in situations that are, let's say, disagreeable?"

"Yes, of course."

"Because I'd like to ask you something rather strange."

"Go ahead."

Jasper Gwyn chose a pastry, he was searching for the right words.

"You see, I recently decided to try to make portraits."

The girl bowed her head almost imperceptibly.

"Naturally I don't know how to paint, and in fact what I have in mind is to *write* portraits. I don't even know myself exactly what that means, but I intend to try it, and I had the idea that I would like to start by making a portrait of you."

The girl remained impassive.

"So what I would like to ask you, Rebecca, is if you would be willing to pose for me, in my studio, pose for a portrait. To get an idea, you could think of what would happen with a painter, or a photographer, it wouldn't be very different, that's the situation, if you can imagine it."

He paused.

"Shall I continue, or would you prefer to stop here?"

The girl leaned slightly toward the table and picked up the coffee cup. But she didn't bring it to her mouth right away.

"Continue," she said.

So Jasper Gwyn explained to her.

"I've taken a studio, behind Marylebone High Street, an enormous, peaceful room. I've put a bed in it, two chairs, not much else. A wooden floor, old walls—a nice place. What I would like is for you to come there, four hours a day for thirty days, from four in the afternoon till eight in the evening. Without skipping a day, not even

Sunday. I would like you to arrive punctually and, whatever happens, stay for four hours, posing, which for me means, simply, being looked at. You won't have to stay in a position that I choose, just be in that room, wherever you'd like, walking or lying down, sitting where you feel like. You won't have to answer questions or talk, and I won't ever ask you to do something particular. Shall I keep going?"

"Yes."

"I'd like you to pose nude, because I think it's an inevitable condition for the success of the portrait."

This he had prepared in front of the mirror. The woman in the rain scarf had honed the words for him.

The girl still had the cup in her hand. Every so often she brought it to her lips but without ever making the decision to drink from it.

Jasper Gwyn took a key out of his pocket and placed it on the table.

"What I'd like is for you to take this key and use it to enter the studio, every day at four in the afternoon. It doesn't matter what I do, you should forget about me. Imagine that you're alone, in there, the whole time. I ask you only to leave precisely at eight in the evening, and lock the door behind you. When we've finished, you'll give me back the key. Drink your coffee, or it will get cold."

The girl looked at the cup she was holding as if she were seeing it for the first time. She put it down on the saucer without drinking.

"Go on," she said. Something had stiffened in her, somewhere.

"I talked to Tom about it. He agreed to give you a leave for those thirty, thirty-five days, at the end of which you'll go back to work at the agency. I know it would be a huge commitment for you, so I propose the sum of five thousand pounds to compensate you for the inconveniences it may cause and for your kindness in putting yourself at my disposal. One last thing, which is important. If you agree, you mustn't talk about it with anyone: it's work that I intend to carry out in the quietest possible way, and I have no interest in having the newspapers or anyone else finding out anything about it. You and Tom and I would be the only ones to know, and for me it's extremely important that it should remain between us. There, I think I've told you everything. I remembered them being better, these pastries."

The girl smiled and turned toward the window. She watched the people passing for a moment, every so often following one with her gaze. Then she stared again at Jasper Gwyn.

"If I do, will I be able to bring books with me?" she asked.

Jasper Gwyn was surprised by his own answer.

"No."

"Music?"

"No. I think you should simply be with yourself, that's all. For an entirely unreasonable time."

The girl nodded, she seemed to understand.

"I suppose," she said, "that the nudity part is pointless to discuss."

"Believe me, it will be more embarrassing for me than for you."

The girl smiled.

"No, it's not that…"

She lowered her head. She smoothed some wrinkles in her skirt.

"The last time someone asked to look at me it didn't go very well."

She made a gesture with her hand, as if she were chasing something away.

"But I've read your books," she said. "You I trust."

Jasper Gwyn smiled at her.

"Would you like to think about it for a few days?"

"No."

She leaned forward and took the key that Jasper Gwyn had placed on the table.

"Let's try," she said.

They sat in silence, with their thoughts, like a couple who have been in love for a long time and no longer need to speak.

That night Jasper Gwyn did something ridiculous, he stood naked in front of the mirror and looked at himself for a long time. He did it because he was sure that Rebecca was doing the same thing, at her house, at that same moment.

The next day they went together to visit the studio. Jasper Gwyn explained to her about the key and everything. He explained to her that he would work with the windows darkened by the wooden shutters and the lights turned on. He insisted that she not turn them off when she went out. He told her he had promised an old man never to do it. She didn't ask him anything, but pointed out that there were no lights. They're about to arrive, said Jasper Gwyn. She lay down on the bed, and stayed there for a while, staring at the ceiling. Jasper Gwyn began to arrange something upstairs, where the bathroom was: he didn't want to be with her, in silence, in that studio, before the time was right. He came down only when he heard her steps on the wooden floor.

Before she left Rebecca gave a last glance around.

"Where will you be?" she asked.

"Forget about me. I don't exist."

Rebecca smiled, and made a face, as if to say yes, she understood, and sooner or later she would get used to it.

They agreed that they could start the following Monday.

25.

Altogether, two years, three months, and twelve days had passed since Jasper Gwyn had communicated to the world that he was going to stop writing. Whatever effect it had had on his public image, he wasn't aware of. The mail went, by a long-standing custom, to Tom, and sometime earlier Jasper Gwyn had asked him not even to send it on, since he had stopped opening it. He rarely read newspapers, he never went on the Internet. In fact, since he had published the list of the fifty-two things he would never do again, Jasper Gwyn had slipped into an isolation that others might have interpreted as a decline but that he tended to experience as a relief. He was convinced that after twelve years of unnatural public exposure, made inevitable by his profession as a writer, he was owed a form of convalescence. He imagined, probably, that when he started to work again, in his new job as a copyist, all the pieces of his life would reawaken and would be reassembled into a newly presentable picture. So when Jasper Gwyn left the house that Monday, it was with the certainty that he was entering not simply into the first day of a new job but into a new period of his existence. This explains why, coming out, he headed resolutely toward his regular barber, with the precise intention of having his head shaved.

He was lucky. It was closed for renovations.

So he wasted a little time and at ten appeared in the workshop of the old man in Camden Town, the one with the light bulbs. They had settled things on the phone. The old man took from a corner an old Italian pasta box that he had sealed with wide green tape and said that it was ready. In the taxi he didn't want to stick it in the trunk, and he held it on his legs the whole way. Given that it was quite a large box but one whose contents were obviously light, there was something eerie about the agility with which he got out of the taxi and went up the few steps that led to Jasper Gwyn's studio.

When he entered he stood still for a moment, without putting down the box.

"I was here once."

"Do you like vintage motorcycles?"

"I don't even know what they are."

They opened the box cautiously and took out the eighteen Catherine de Médicis. They were wrapped individually in very soft tissue paper. Jasper Gwyn got the ladder he had bought from an Indian around the corner and then stepped out of the way. The old man took an unreasonably long time, by moving the ladder, and climbing up, and climbing down, but in the end he achieved the hoped-for effect of eighteen Catherine de Médicis installed in eighteen sockets hanging from the ceiling in a geometric arrangement. Even turned off they made a good show.

"Will you turn them on?" asked Jasper Gwyn, after closing the shutters on the windows.

"Yes, it would be better," the old man said, as if an inexact pressure on the switch could possibly compromise everything.

Probably, in his sick artisan's mind, it did.

He approached the electrical panel, and with his gaze fixed on his bulbs pressed the switch.

They were silent for a moment.

"Did I tell you I wanted red?" asked Jasper Gwyn, bewildered.

"Quiet."

For some reason that Jasper Gwyn was unable to understand, the light bulbs, which went on in a brilliant red color that transformed the studio into a bordello, slowly faded until they stabilized at a shade between amber and blue that could not be described as anything other than *childlike*.

The old man muttered something, satisfied.

"Incredible," said Jasper Gwyn. He was genuinely moved.

Before leaving, he turned on the system that David Barber had prepared for him, and in the big room a current of sounds began to flow that apparently dragged along, at an astonishingly slow rate, piles of dry leaves and hazy harmonies of children's wind instruments. Jasper Gwyn gave a last glance around. It was all ready.

"Not to pry into your business, but what do you do in here?" asked the old man.

"I work. I'm a copyist."

The old man nodded. He was noticing that there was no desk in the room and, instead, a bed and two armchairs were visible. But he knew that every craftsman has his particular style.

"I once knew someone who was a copyist" was all he said.

They didn't go into it further.

They ate together, in a pub across the street. When they said goodbye, with dignified warmth, it was two forty-five. Rebecca would arrive in just a little over an hour, and Jasper Gwyn prepared to do what he had been planning, in detail, for days.

26.

He headed toward the Underground, took the Bakerloo line, got out at Charing Cross, and for a couple of hours browsed some used-book stores, seeking, without finding, a handbook on the use of inks. By chance he bought a biography of Rebecca West, and stole an eighteenth-century anthology of haiku, hiding it in his pocket. Around five he went into a café because he needed a bathroom. At the table, drinking a whiskey, he paged through the anthology of haiku, wondering for the hundredth time what sort of mind you needed to pursue a type of beauty like that. When he realized that it was already six, he left and went to a small organic supermarket in the neighborhood, where he bought four things for dinner. Then he went to the nearest tube station, stopping to visit a Laundromat that he came across on the way: he'd been cultivating the idea of compiling a guide to the hundred best places to do your laundry in London, so he never missed an opportunity to bring himself up to date. He got home at seven twenty. He took a shower, put on a Billie Holiday record, and cooked dinner, reheating on a slow flame some lentil soup, which he buried under grated parmesan. After he ate, he left the dishes on the table and stretched out on the couch, choosing the three books that he would devote the evening to. They were a Bolaño novel, the complete Donald Duck stories by Carl Barks, and Descartes's *Discourse on Method*. At least two of the three had changed the world. At nine fifteen the telephone rang. Usually Jasper Gwyn didn't answer, but it was a special day.

"Hello?"

"Hello, it's Rebecca."

"Good evening, Rebecca."

A long moment of silence slid by.

"I'm sorry if I'm disturbing you. I just wanted to say that I went to the studio today."

"I was sure of it."

"Because I began to wonder if I'd got the day wrong."

"No, no, it was today."

"Okay, good, I can go to bed in peace."

"Certainly."

Another gust of silence went by.

"I went and I did what you told me to."

"Very good. You didn't turn off the lights, right?"

"No, I left everything as it was."

"Perfect. See you tomorrow."

"Yes."

"Good night, Rebecca."

"Good night. And I'm sorry if I bothered you."

Jasper Gwyn went back to reading. He was in the middle of a fantastic story. Donald Duck was a traveling salesman and had been sent to the wilds of Alaska. He scaled mountains and jour-neyed down rivers, always carrying a sample of his wares. The great thing was the type of wares he was supposed to sell: pipe organs.

Then he went on to Descartes.

27.

But the next day he was there when Rebecca arrived.

He was sitting on the floor, leaning against the wall. In the studio David Barber's loop was playing. A slow river.

Rebecca greeted him with a cautious smile. Jasper Gwyn nodded. He was wearing a light jacket and had chosen for the occasion leather shoes, with laces, pale brown. They gave an impression of seriousness. Of work.

When Rebecca began to undress he got up to reposition the shutters at one of the windows, mainly because it seemed to him inelegant to stand there watching her. She left her clothes on a chair. The last thing she took off was a black T-shirt. Under it she wore nothing. She went to sit on the bed. Her skin was very white; she had a tattoo at the base of her spine.

Jasper Gwyn sat down again on the floor, where he had been before, and began to look. Her small breasts surprised him, and the secret moles, but it wasn't on the details that he wanted to linger—it was more urgent to understand the whole, to bring back to some unity that figure which, for reasons to be clarified, seemed to have no coherence. He thought that without clothes it gave the impression of a random figure. He almost immediately lost the sense of time, and the simple act of observing seemed natural to him. Every so often he lowered his gaze, as another might have come back to the surface, to breathe.

For a long time Rebecca stayed on the bed. Then Jasper Gwyn saw her get up and slowly pace the room, taking small steps. She kept her eyes on the floor, and looked for imaginary points where she could place her feet, which were like a child's. She moved as if each time she were assembling pieces of herself that were not intended to stay together. Her body seemed to be the result of an effort of will.

She returned to the bed. She lay down on her back, her neck resting on the pillow. She kept her eyes open.

At eight she got dressed, and for a few minutes sat, with her raincoat on, on a chair, breathing. Then she got up and left—just a small nod of goodbye.

For a moment Jasper Gwyn didn't move. When he got up, he did so in order to lie down on the bed. He began to stare at the ceiling. He rested his head in the indentation in the pillow left by Rebecca.

"How did it go?" asked the woman with the rain scarf.

"I don't know."

"She's good, the girl."

"I'm not sure she'll come back."

"Why not?"

"It's all so ridiculous."

"So?"

"I'm not even sure I'll go back myself."

But the next day he returned.

28.

It occurred to him to bring a notebook. He chose one that wasn't too small, its pages cream-colored. With a pencil, every so often he wrote down some words, then he tore out the page and fastened it with a thumbtack to the wooden floor, each time choosing a different place, like someone setting out mousetraps.

So he wrote a sentence, at a certain point, and then he wandered around the room until he chose a point, on the floor, not far from where Rebecca was at that moment, standing, leaning against a wall. He bent over and fastened it to the wood with the thumbtack. Then he looked up at Rebecca. He had never been so close to her, since they started. Rebecca was staring into his eyes. They remained staring like that. They breathed slowly, in the river of David Barber's sounds. Then Jasper Gwyn lowered his gaze.

Before she left, Rebecca crossed the room and went right over to where Jasper Gwyn was huddled, sitting on the floor, in a corner. She sat down beside him, stretching out her legs and hiding her hands between her thighs, with the backs touching. She didn't turn to look at him, she just stayed there, her head leaning against the wall. Jasper Gwyn then felt her warm closeness, and her perfume. He did so until Rebecca got up, dressed, and went out.

Left alone, Jasper Gwyn noted something on his pieces of paper and pinned them to the floor, at points that he chose with minute attention.

29.

Rebecca got in the habit of walking around those pieces of paper, on the days that followed, designing routes that took her from one to another, as if she were seeking the outline of some figure. She never stopped to read them, she just walked around them. Slowly Jasper Gwyn saw her change, become different in her ways of revealing herself, more unexpected in her movements. Perhaps it was the seventh day, or the eighth, when he saw her suddenly composed into a surprising beauty, without flaw. It lasted a moment, as if she knew very well how far she had ventured, and had no intention of staying there. So she shifted her weight onto the other side, raising a hand to smooth her hair, and becoming imperfect again.

That same day, she began to murmur, in a low voice, as she lay on the bed. Jasper Gwyn couldn't hear the words, and didn't want to. But she went on for many minutes, every so often smiling, or pausing in silence, and then starting up again. She seemed to be telling someone something. As she spoke she slid the palms of her hands back and forth along her extended legs. She stopped when she was silent. Without even realizing it, Jasper Gwyn approached the bed, like someone who is pursuing a small animal and ends up a few steps from its den. She didn't react, she only lowered the tone of her voice, and continued to speak, but barely moving her lips, in a whisper that sometimes ceased, and then began again.

The next day, while Jasper Gwyn was looking at her, her eyes filled with tears, but it was a moment of transient thoughts or of memories in flight.

If Jasper Gwyn had had to say when he began to think that there was a solution, probably he would have cited a day when, at a certain point, she put on her shirt, and it wasn't a way of going back on some decision but of going forward beyond what she had decided. She kept it on but unbuttoned in the front—she played with the cuffs. Then something in her shifted, in a way that one might have defined as *lateral*, and Jasper Gwyn felt, for the first time, that Rebecca was letting him glimpse her true portrait.

That night he went out and walked the streets, and he walked for hours, without feeling fatigue. He observed that there were Laundromats that never closed, and he registered the fact with a particular satisfaction.

30.

He no longer saw her as fat, or beautiful, and whatever he had thought and learned about her, before entering that studio, had completely dissipated, or had never existed. As it seemed to him that time did not pass in there but that, rather, a single instant unrolled, always identical to itself. He began to recognize, sometimes, passages in David Barber's loop, and their periodic returns, which were always the same, gave any lapse of time a poetic fixity compared to which what was happening in the world outside lost any enchantment. That everything took shape in a single unchanging, childish light was an infinite joy. The odors of the studio, the dust that was lying on things, the dirt that no one resisted—everything gave the impression of an animal in hibernation, breathing slowly, dead to the world. To the woman with the rain scarf, who wanted to know, Jasper Gwyn went so far as to explain that there was something hypnotic in all that, similar to the effects of a drug. I wouldn't exaggerate, said the old woman. And she reminded him that it was, after all, only a job, the job of a copyist. Think rather of accomplishing something good, she added, otherwise you'll be right back to meeting with students.

"How many days left?" asked Jasper Gwyn.

"Twenty, I think."

"I have time."

"Have you already written something?"

"Notes. Nothing it would make sense to read."

"If I were you I wouldn't be so calm."

"I'm not calm. I said only that I have time. I was thinking of panicking in a few days."

"Always putting things off, you young people."

31.

He often arrived late, when Rebecca was already in the studio. It might be ten minutes, or it might be an hour. He did it deliberately. He liked to find that she had already disappeared to herself in David Barber's sound river and in that light—when he, instead, was still immersed in the crudeness and the rhythm of the world outside. Then he entered, making as little noise as possible, and on the threshold stopped, searching for her with his gaze as if in a giant birdcage: the instant he found her—that was the image that would remain most distinct in his memory. In time she got used to it, and didn't move when the door opened, but just stayed where she was. For days now they had been omitting any useless liturgy of greeting or farewell, in meeting and parting.

One day he came in and Rebecca was sleeping. Lying on the bed, slightly turned onto one side. She was breathing slowly. Jasper Gwyn silently approached a chair at the foot of the bed. He sat down and watched her for a long time. As he had never done before, he scrutinized the details from close up, the folds of the body, the shadings of white in the skin, the small things. He didn't care about fixing them in his memory, they wouldn't be useful in his portrait, but by means of that looking he gained a secret closeness that in fact did help, and carried him far. He let the time pass without rushing the ideas he felt arriving, scattered and disorderly like people coming from a border. At some point Rebecca opened her eyes, saw him. Instinctively she closed her legs. But slowly she reopened them, returning to the position she had abandoned—she stared at him for a few seconds, and then closed her eyes again.

Jasper Gwyn didn't move from the chair, that day, and he got so close to Rebecca that it was natural to end up where she was, first passing through a torpor full of images, then sliding into sleep, without resisting, slumped in the chair. The last thing he heard was the voice of the woman in the rain scarf. Fine way of working, she said.

On the other hand it seemed normal to Rebecca, when she opened her eyes—something that was bound to happen. The writer asleep. What a strange sweetness. Silently she got off the bed. It was past eight. Before getting dressed she approached Jasper Gwyn and stood looking at him. She walked around him, and since one elbow was resting on the arm of the chair, the hand hanging in space, she brought her hips close to that hand, almost touching it, and stood motionless for a moment—the fingers of that man and my sex, she thought. She got dressed without making any noise. He was still sleeping when she left.

As she did every evening, she took her first steps on the street with the tentativeness of a newborn animal.

32.

When she got home there was a guy.

"Hi, Rebecca," he said.

"I told you to let me know when you're coming back here."

But without even taking off her coat she kissed him.

Later, at night, Rebecca told him she had a new job. I'm posing for a painter, she said.

"You?"

"Yes, me."

He laughed.

"Nude," she said.

"Come on."

"It's not a bad job. Every day, four hours a day."

"Shit, why'd you do it?"

"Money. He's giving me five thousand pounds. We have to pay for the flat somehow. Are you going to do it?"

The guy was a photographer, but not many people seemed disposed to believe it. So Rebecca took care of everything, the rent, the bills, the stuff in the fridge. He every so often disappeared, then he returned. His things were there. Rebecca usually summed up the situation in very elementary terms. I'm in love with a shit, she said.

A couple of months earlier, he had said that a friend of his wanted to take some photographs of her. They arranged to meet one evening, there at her house. They drank a lot and eventually Rebecca found herself naked on the bed, with the friend taking snapshots. At some point her boyfriend the shit undressed and came over to her. They had begun to make love. The friend meanwhile took pictures. Then, for a few days, Rebecca hadn't wanted to see the shit. But not even then had she stopped loving him.

She knew, besides, that she was destined by her body to ridiculous loves. No man thinks he desires a body like that. But experience had taught Rebecca that, in fact, many desire it, and it's often the result of some wound they don't want to admit. Often they are afraid of the female body, without knowing it. Sometimes they need to despise it to get excited, and then possessing that body makes them feel good. Almost always there was a sort of expectation of perversion in the air, as if to choose that anomalous beauty necessarily involved giving up the simpler and more straightforward modes of desire. So, at twenty-seven, Rebecca already had a pile of bad memories, where she would have had a hard time finding the simple sweetness of a clean, pure moment. It didn't matter to her. There wasn't much she could do, in that regard.

So she stayed with her shit boyfriend. So she wasn't surprised when Jasper Gwyn had made her that offer. It was exactly the sort of thing she had learned to expect from life.

33.

In the morning she left the shit boyfriend asleep in the bed and went out without even taking a shower. She had a night of sex on her, and she liked carrying it around with her, completely. Today you'll get me like this, dear Jasper Gwyn, let's see what effect it has on you.

For four hours, every morning, she still went to work for Tom. She revered that man. Three years earlier, a car accident had confined him to a wheelchair, and he had built up around himself an enormous office, a kind of country, where he was God. He was surrounded by workers of all kinds, some very old, some completely mad. He was always stuck to the telephone. He paid little and seldom, but that was a detail. He had such energy, and generated so much life, that people adored him. He was the sort of person who, if you happened to die, would take it as a personal insult.

About the matter of the portrait he had never said anything to her. Only once, when Rebecca had been going to Jasper Gwyn's for several days, he had come by in his wheelchair and, stopping in front of her desk, had said:

"If I ask you something, tell me to fuck off."

"Okay."

"How is old Jasper behaving?"

"Fuck off."

"Perfect."

So at one o'clock she got up, took her stuff, and, on the way out, said goodbye to Tom. They both knew where she was going, but they pretended it was nothing. Every so often he glanced at how she was dressed. Maybe he thought he could deduce something from that, who knows.

She went to Jasper Gwyn's studio on the Underground, but she always got out one stop earlier, to walk a little before going in. On the street, she turned the key over and over in her hand. And that was her way of starting work. Another thing she did was to think in what order she would take her clothes off. It was strange, but, being close to that man every single day, she had learned a sort of precision in her gestures that she had never imagined necessary.

He led you to believe that everything wasn't equivalent, and that someone, somewhere, was recording our every action—one day, likely, he would ask us to account for it.

She turned the key in the lock and entered.

She couldn't tell right away if he was already there. She had learned that it wasn't important. Yet she didn't feel safe until she saw him—or tranquil until he was looking at her. She could never have imagined it before, but really the most ridiculous thing—that that man should stare at her—had become the thing she needed, and without which she could find nothing of herself. She realized, to her surprise, that she was aware of being naked only when she was alone, or he wasn't looking at her. Whereas it seemed natural when he stared at her; she felt clothed, then, and complete, like a job well done. As the days passed, she was startled to find herself wishing that he would get closer, and often the way he stayed leaning against the wall frustrated her, his reluctance to take what she would have granted him without any trouble. Then it might happen that she approached him, but it wasn't simple, you had to be capable of avoiding any position that might seem a seduction—the gesture ended up being brusque, and inexact. It was always he who regained a painless distance.

The day she arrived with her night of sex on her, Jasper Gwyn didn't show up. Rebecca had time to calculate: eighteen days had passed since they began. She thought that the number of bulbs hanging from the ceiling was also eighteen. Mad as he was, it was even possible that Jasper Gwyn attributed some meaning to the circumstance—maybe that was why he hadn't come. She got dressed, exactly at eight, and then she took a long time getting home—it was as if she expected that something should first be restored to her.

34.

Jasper Gwyn didn't arrive the next day, either. Rebecca felt the hours pass exasperatingly slowly. She was sure he would appear, but he didn't, and when she got dressed, exactly at eight, she did it angrily. In the evening, walking along the street, she thought she was a fool, it was only a job, what did it matter to her—but she also tried to remember if she had read anything strange in him, the last time they had seen each other. She remembered him bent over his pages, nothing else.

The next day she arrived late, on purpose—just a few minutes, but for Jasper Gwyn, she knew, it was an enormity. She went in, and the studio was deserted. Rebecca got undressed but she couldn't find the cynicism, or the simplicity, not to think of anything; she spent the time measuring her increasing anxiety. She couldn't do what she was supposed to do—be herself, simply—although she recalled clearly how easy it had seemed, the first day, when he hadn't shown up. Evidently something must have happened—like a journey. Now there was nowhere to go back to; besides, no path seemed possible without him.

You're a fool, she thought.

He must be sick. He must be working at home. Maybe he's finished. Maybe he's *dead*.

But she knew it wasn't true, because Jasper Gwyn was a precise man, even in error.

She lay down on the bed, and for the first time she seemed to have an inkling of fear, being there by herself. She tried to remember if she had locked the door. She wondered if she was sure that three days had passed since she had seen him last. She went through in her memory those three afternoons full of nothing. It seemed to her even worse. Relax, she thought. He'll arrive, she said to herself. She closed her eyes. She began to caress herself, first her body, slowly, then between her legs. She wasn't thinking of anything in particular, and that did her good. She turned slightly onto one side, because that was how she liked to do it. She opened her eyes again, in front of her was the door. He'll open it and I won't stop, she thought. He doesn't exist, I exist, and this is what I feel like doing now, dear Jasper Gwyn. I feel like caressing myself. Just come in that door, and then we'll see what you feel like writing. I'll keep going, until the end, I don't care if you look. She closed her eyes again.

At eight she got up, dressed, and went home. She thought that there were ten days left, maybe a few more. She couldn't understand if it was a little or a lot. It was a tiny eternity.

35.

The next day when she entered the room Jasper Gwyn was sitting on a chair, in a corner. He seemed like the guard in a museum gallery, watching over a work of contemporary art.

Instinctively Rebecca stiffened. She looked questioningly at Jasper Gwyn. He merely stared at her. Then, for the first time since they'd started, she spoke.

"You haven't been here for three days," she said.

Then she became aware of the other man. He was standing in a corner, leaning against the wall.

Two men, there was another, sitting on the first step of the stairs that led to the bathroom.

Rebecca raised her voice and said it wasn't in the agreement, but without clarifying what she was referring to. She said also that she considered herself free to stop when she liked, and that if he thought that for five thousand pounds he could dare to do anything he wanted he was grossly mistaken. Then she stayed there, motionless, because Jasper Gwyn did not look like he wanted to answer.

"What a shit," she said, but to herself more than anything.

She sat on the bed, dressed, and stayed there, for quite a while.

There was that music by David Barber.

She decided not to be afraid.

If anything, they should be afraid of her.

She undressed brusquely, and began to walk around the room. She stayed far away from Jasper Gwyn, but passed close to the other two men, without looking at them. Where the hell did he get them, she thought. And with her footsteps she trampled Jasper Gwyn's pieces of paper, first by walking over them, then tearing them with the soles of her feet; she felt the hardness of the thumbtacks scratching her skin—she didn't care. She chose some and destroyed them—others she allowed to survive. She thought that she was like a servant who extinguishes the candles at night, throughout the palace, and leaves some lighted, because of some house rule. She liked the idea and gradually stopped doing it angrily, and began to do it with the meekness that would be expected from that servant. She slowed down, and her gaze lost its harshness. She continued to extinguish those pieces of paper, but with a different, gentle care. When it seemed to her that she had finished—whatever it was she had begun—she lay down on the bed again, and let her head sink into the pillow, closing her eyes. She was no longer angry, and in fact was amazed to feel a sort of peace coming over her that, she understood, she had been expecting for days. Nothing moved around her, but at some point there was some movement, footsteps, and then the sharp sound of a chair, maybe several chairs, being dragged next to the bed. She didn't open her eyes, she had no need to know. She let herself subside into a mute darkness, and that darkness was herself. She could do it, and without fear, and easily, because someone was looking at her—she immediately realized it. For some reason that she didn't understand, she was finally alone, in a perfect way, as one never is—or rarely, she thought, in a loving embrace. She was far away, having lost any notion of time, perhaps almost sleeping, sometimes wondering if those two men would touch her—and the third man, the only one for whom she was really there.

She opened her eyes, afraid that it was late. In the room there was no one. Next to the bed was a chair, only one. Leaving, she touched it. Slowly, with the back of her hand.

36.

When she entered the studio, at precisely four the next day, the first thing she saw was Jasper Gwyn's pages, back in their places, not even a crease, restored again, with the thumbtacks and all. There were hundreds by now. It didn't seem that anyone had ever walked on them. Rebecca looked up and Jasper Gwyn was there, sitting on the floor, in what seemed to have become his den, his back leaning against the wall. Everything was in its place, the light, the music, the bed. The chairs lined up on one side of the room, in order, except the one that he used every so often, placed in a corner, the notebook on the floor. That sensation of safety, she thought—which I never knew before.

She undressed, took a chair, moved it to a point she liked, not too close to Jasper Gwyn, not too far, and sat down. They stayed like that for a long time. Jasper Gwyn every so often looked at her, but more often stared at something in the room, making small gestures in the air, as if he were following some music. He seemed to miss his notebook, his eyes searched for it a couple of times, but in reality he didn't get up to find it, he felt like staying there, leaning against the wall. Until, unexpectedly, Rebecca started talking.

"Tonight I thought of something," she said.

Jasper Gwyn turned to look at her, caught by surprise.

"Yes, I know, I shouldn't talk, I'll stop right away."

Her voice was calm, serene.

"But there's a stupid thing I've decided to do. I don't even know if I'm doing it for me or for you, I mean only that it seems right, the way here the light is right, the music, everything is right, except one thing. So I've decided to do it."

She got up, went over to Jasper Gwyn, and knelt in front of him.

"I know, it's stupid, I'm sorry. But let me do it."

And, as she would have done with a child, she leaned toward him and slowly took off his jacket. Jasper Gwyn did not resist. He seemed reassured by seeing Rebecca fold the jacket in the proper way and place it carefully on the floor. Then she unbuttoned his shirt, leaving the buttons of the cuffs for last. She took it off, and again folded it in an orderly way, placing it on the jacket. She seemed satisfied, and for a little while she didn't move. Then she moved back, and leaned over to unlace Jasper Gwyn's shoes. She took them off. Jasper Gwyn drew his feet back because all men are embarrassed about socks. But she smiled, and took those off, too. She put everything in order, as he would have done, taking care that it was all lined up.

She looked at Jasper Gwyn and said it was much better this way.

"It's much more precise," she said.

She got up and went to sit in the chair again. It was stupid, but her heart was pounding as if she had run a race—it was exactly as she had imagined it, at night, when it had occurred to her.

Jasper Gwyn began looking around again, went back to making small gestures in the air. Nothing seemed to have changed for him. As if he had suddenly become an animal, Rebecca thought, however. She looked at his thin chest, his skinny arms, and returned to a time when Jasper Gwyn was to her a distant writer, a photograph, some interviews—entire evenings reading him, rapt. She remembered the first time Tom had sent her to the Laundromat, with that cell phone. It had seemed crazy to her, and then Tom had paused to explain a little what sort of person Jasper Gwyn was. He had told her that in his last book there was a dedication. Maybe she remembered: *To P., farewell.* He explained that "P." stood for Paul, who was a child. He was four, and Jasper Gwyn was his father. But they had never seen each other, simply because Jasper Gwyn had decided that he would never be a father, and for no reason. He was able to sustain it with great sweetness and determination. And he told her something else. There were at least two other books by

Jasper Gwyn that circulated in the world, but not under his name, and certainly it wasn't he who would tell her what they were. Then Tom had pointed a blue ballpoint pen at his head and had made a noise with his mouth, like a puff of air.

"It's a destroyer of memory," he had explained. "You don't know anything."

She had taken the cell phone and gone to the Laundromat. She remembered him very well, that man, sitting in the midst of the washing machines, elegant, his hands forgotten on his knees. He had seemed a sort of divinity, because she was still young, and it was the first time. At a certain point he had tried to tell her something about Tom and a refrigerator, but she had had trouble concentrating, because he spoke without looking in her eyes, and in a voice that she seemed to have known forever.

Now the man was here, with his thin chest, his skinny arms, his bare feet placed one on top of the other—an elegant, princely animal relict. Rebecca thought how far one can go, and how mysterious are the pathways of experience if they can lead you to be sitting on a chair, naked, observed by a man who has dragged his folly here from far away, rearranging it to make a refuge for him and for you. It occurred to her that every time she had read a page by him she had been invited into that refuge, and that basically nothing had happened since then, absolutely nothing—maybe a belated alignment of bodies, always late.

From then on Jasper Gwyn, when he worked, wore only a pair of old mechanic's pants. It gave him something of the air of a mad painter, and this didn't do any harm.

37.

Days passed, and one afternoon a light bulb went out. The old man of Camden Town had done well. It went without a flicker and silent as a memory.

Rebecca turned to look at it—she was sitting on the bed, it was like an imperceptible oscillation of the space. She felt a pang of anguish; it was impossible not to. Jasper Gwyn had explained to her how it would all end, and now she knew what would happen, but not how fast, or how slowly. She had long ago stopped counting days, and she always refused to ask herself how it would be afterward. She was afraid to ask herself.

Jasper Gwyn got up, walked under the bulb that had gone out, and began to observe it, with an interest that one would have called scientific. He didn't seem worried. He seemed to be wondering why that particular one. Rebecca smiled. She thought that if he wasn't afraid, she wouldn't be afraid, either. She sat on the bed and from there saw Jasper Gwyn walk around the studio, his head bent, for the first time interested in those pieces of paper he had pinned to the floor and had never looked at again. He picked up one, then another. He took out the thumbtack, picked up the piece of paper, put it in his pocket, and then put the thumbtack on a windowsill, always the same one. The thing absorbed his attention completely, and Rebecca realized that she could even have left and he wouldn't have noticed. When the second bulb went out, they both turned to look at it, for a moment. It was like waiting for shooting stars on a summer night. At some point Jasper Gwyn seemed to remember something, and then he went to lower the volume on David

Barber's loop. With his hand on the control knob, he stared at the bulbs, seeking a mathematical symmetry.

That day Rebecca went home and said to the shit boyfriend could he please leave, just for a few days—she said she would like to be alone, for a while. And where should I go? asked the shit boyfriend. Anywhere, she said.

The next day she didn't even go to work for Tom.

It had occurred to her that something was ending, and she wanted to do it well, she wanted to do only that.

Jasper Gwyn must have had a similar idea, because when she arrived at the studio the next day, she saw the remains of a dinner, in a corner, on the floor, and understood that Jasper Gwyn had not gone home at night—nor would he before it was all finished. She thought how exact that man was.

38.

Every so often as she walked she passed through the patches of darkness, as if to try out disappearance. Jasper Gwyn watched her, waiting for something from the shadows. Then he returned to his thoughts. He seemed happy, tranquil, amid the remains of his dinners, his face unshaved, his hair disheveled from nights on the floor. Rebecca looked at him and thought he was irrevocably charming. Who knew if he had found what he was looking for? It wasn't possible to read in his face any satisfaction or a hint of distress. Only the traces of a feverish but peaceful concentration. Some pieces of paper picked up from the floor—then he crumpled them up and put them in his pocket. His gaze on the light bulbs, the instant they gave up.

But at a certain point he came and sat next to her, on the bed, and, as if it were the most natural thing in the world, he began talking to her.

"You see, Rebecca, there's one thing I seem to have understood."

She waited.

"I thought that not speaking was absolutely necessary, I have a horror of chat, I certainly couldn't think of chatting with you. And then I was afraid it would end up as something like psychoanalysis, or confession. A terrible prospect, don't you think?"

Rebecca smiled.

"However, you see, I was wrong," Jasper Gwyn added.

He was silent for a moment.

"The truth is that if I really want to do this job I have to agree to talk, even just once, twice at most, at the right moment, but I have to be capable of doing it."

He looked up at Rebecca.

"Just barely talk," he said.

She nodded yes. She was sitting completely naked next to a man in mechanic's pants, and it seemed to her utterly natural. The only thing she wondered was how she could be useful to that man.

"For example, before it's too late, I'd like to ask you something," said Jasper Gwyn.

"Go on."

Jasper Gwyn asked her. She thought about it, then answered. It was a question about crying and laughing.

They went on talking about it for a while.

Then he asked her something about children. Sons and daughters, he explained.

And something else about landscapes.

They talked in low voices, without hurrying.

Until he nodded and got up.

"Thank you," he said.

Then he added that it hadn't been so difficult. He appeared to say it to himself, but he also turned toward Rebecca, as if he expected some sort of response.

"No, it wasn't difficult," she said then. She said that nothing, there, was difficult.

Jasper Gwyn went to regulate the volume of the music, and David Barber's loop seemed to disappear into the walls, leaving behind little more than a wake, in the fragile light of the last six light bulbs.

39.

They waited for the last one in silence, on the thirty-sixth day of that strange experiment. At eight o'clock, it seemed to be taken for granted that they would wait together, because the only time that counted anymore was written into the copper filaments produced by the mad talent of the old man in Camden Town.

In the light of the last two bulbs, the studio was already a black sack, kept alive by two pupils of light. When the last remained, it was a whisper.

They looked at it from a distance, without approaching, so as not to defile it.

It was night, and it went out.

Through the darkened windows came just enough light to mark the edges of things, and not right away, but only to eyes accustomed to the darkness.

Every object appeared finished, and only the two of them still living.

Rebecca had never known such intensity. She thought that at that moment any movement would be unsuitable, but she understood that the opposite was also true, that it was impossible, at that moment, to make a wrong movement. So she imagined many things; some she had begun to imagine long before. Until she heard the voice of Jasper Gwyn.

"I think I'll wait for the morning light in here. But you can go, of course, Rebecca."

He said it with a kind of tenderness that might also seem to be regret, so Rebecca came over to him and when she found the right words she said that she would like to stay and wait there with him—just that.

But Jasper Gwyn said nothing and she understood.

She got dressed slowly, for the last time, and when she was at the door she stopped.

"I'm sure I should say something special, but, truthfully, nothing really occurs to me."

Jasper Gwyn smiled in the darkness.

"Don't worry, it's a phenomenon I'm very well acquainted with."

They shook hands as they said goodbye, and the gesture seemed to them both to have a memorable precision and foolishness.

40.

Jasper Gwyn spent five days writing the portrait—he did it at home, on the computer, going out from time to time to walk, or eat something. As he worked he listened to Frank Sinatra records over and over.

When he thought he had finished, he copied the file onto a CD and took it to a printer. He chose square sheets of a rather heavy laid paper, and a blue ink that was almost black. He laid out the pages in such a way that they looked airy without seeming trivial. After long reflection, he chose a font that perfectly imitated the letters made by a typewriter: in the roundness of the *o* there was a hint of blurring in the ink. He didn't want any binding. He had two copies made. At the end the printer was noticeably worn out.

The next day Jasper Gwyn spent hours looking for a tissue paper that seemed to him appropriate, and a folder, with a tie, that wasn't too big, or too small, or too much folder. He found both in a stationer's that was about to close, after eighty-six years in business, and was getting rid of its stock.

"Why are you closing?" he asked at the cash register.

"The owner is retiring," a woman with nondescript hair answered, without emotion.

"Doesn't he have children?" Jasper Gwyn persisted.

The woman looked up.

"I'm the child," she said.

"I see."

"Do you want a gift bag or is it for you?"

"It's a gift for me."

The woman gave a sigh that could mean many things. She took the price off the folder and put everything in an elegant envelope fastened with a thin gold string. Then she said that her grandfather had opened that shop when he returned from the First World War, investing everything he had. He had never closed it, not even during the bombing in 1940. He claimed to have invented the system of sealing envelopes by licking the edge. But probably, she added, that was nonsense.

Jasper Gwyn paid.

"You don't find envelopes like this anymore," he said.

"My grandfather made them with a strawberry taste," she said.

"Seriously?"

"So he said. Lemon and strawberry, people didn't want the lemon ones, who knows why. I remember trying them as a child. They didn't taste like anything. They tasted like glue."

"You'll take the stationery store," Jasper Gwyn said then.

"No. I want to sing."

"Really? Opera?"

"Tangos."

"Tangos?"

"Tangos."

"Fantastic."

"And what do you do?"

"Copyist."

"Fantastic."

41.

That night Jasper Gwyn re-read the seven square pages that contained, in two columns, the text of the portrait. The idea was to then wrap the pages in the tissue paper and put them in the folder with the tie. At that point the work would be finished.

"How does it seem to you?"

"Really not bad," answered the woman with the rain scarf.

"Be truthful."

"I am. You wanted to make a portrait and you did. Frankly I wouldn't have bet a cent."

"No?"

"No. Write a portrait? What sort of idea is that? But now I've read your seven pages and I know it's an idea that exists. You've found a way of making it into a real object. And I have to admit that you've found a simple and brilliant system. Well done."

"It's thanks to you, too."

"What?"

"A long time ago, maybe you don't remember, you told me that if I really had to be a copyist I should at least try to copy people, not numbers, or medical reports."

"Of course I remember. It's the only time in my life we met."

"You said that it would suit me very well. Copying people, I mean. You said it with an assurance that had no nuances, as if there were no need even to discuss it."

"So?"

"I don't think this idea of the portraits would have occurred to me if you hadn't said that phrase. In that way. I'm sincere: I wouldn't be here without you."

The woman turned to him and she had the face of an old teacher who hears the doorbell ring and it's that coward from the second row who has come to thank her, the day he graduates. She made a gesture like a caress, looking in the other direction, however.

"You're a good boy," she said.

They were silent for a while. The woman with the rain scarf took out a big handkerchief and blew her nose. Then she placed a hand on Jasper Gwyn's arm.

"There's one thing I never told you," she said. "Do you want to hear it?"

"Of course."

"That day, when you brought me home... I kept thinking of how you didn't want to write books anymore, I couldn't get it out of my mind that it was a damn shame. I wasn't even sure if I had asked you why, or anyway I didn't remember if you had really explained why in the world you no longer wanted anything to do with it. In other words, I felt something was still not right, you understand?"

"Yes."

"It lasted several days. Then one morning I go as usual to the Indian downstairs and see the cover of a magazine. There was a whole pile of that magazine, just arrived, they had put it under the cheese potato chips. In that issue they had interviewed a writer, so on the cover there was his name and a statement, his name nice and big and this statement in quotation marks. And the statement said: 'In love we all lie.' I swear. And, note, he was a great writer, I could be wrong but I think he was even a Nobel winner. Also on the cover was an actress not quite undressed, who promised to tell the whole truth. I don't remember about what stupid thing."

She was silent for a while, as if she were trying to remember it. But then she said something else.

"It doesn't mean anything, I know, but you moved your hand a few inches and you could grab the cheese potato chips."

She hesitated a second.

"In love we all lie," she murmured, shaking her head. Then she shouted the next sentence.

"Well done, Mr. Gwyn!"

She said she had begun to shout right there at the Indian's, with people turning. She had repeated it three or four times.

"Well done, Mr. Gwyn!"

They had thought she was mad.

"But it's happened to me often," she said. "To be thought mad," she clarified.

Then Jasper Gwyn said there was no one like her, and asked if she would like to celebrate somewhere together, that night.

"Excuse me?"

"What do you say to having dinner with me?"

"Don't talk nonsense, I'm dead, restaurants hate me."

"At least a glass."

"What sort of idea is that?"

"Do it for me."

"Now it's really time to go."

She said it in a gentle voice, but firm. She got up, took her purse and her umbrella, which was still wet, and went toward the door. She dragged her feet a little, in that way of hers, so that you could recognize it from a distance. When she stopped it was because she still had something to say.

"Don't be rude, take those seven pages to Rebecca, and make her read them."

"You think it's necessary?"

"Of course."

"What will she say?"

"It's me, she'll say."

Jasper Gwyn wondered if he would ever see her again and decided that he would, somewhere, but not for many years, and in a different solitude.

42.

He was in a new Laundromat that some Pakistanis had opened behind his house when a boy in a jacket and tie approached; he couldn't have been more than twenty.

"Are you Jasper Gwyn?"

"No."

"Yes, you are," said the boy, and handed him a cell phone. "It's for you."

Jasper Gwyn took it, resigned. But also somewhat glad.

"Hey, Tom."

"You know how many days since I've phoned you, big brother?"

"You tell me."

"Forty-one."

"A record."

"You can say that again. How's the Laundromat?"

"Just opened, you know how it is."

"No, I don't know, Lottie does the washing."

They had an open bet, and so after tossing a lot of nonsense back and forth they reached it. It was the question of the portrait.

"Rebecca doesn't cough up anything, so it's up to you to tell, Jasper. I want the details, too."

"Here in the Laundromat?"

"Why not?"

In fact there was no reason not to talk about it. Apart from that boy in the jacket and tie, perhaps, who remained, stiffly, in the way. Jasper Gwyn gave him a look and he understood. He went out of the Laundromat.

"I did it. It came out well."

"The portrait?"

"Yes."

"It came out well in what sense?"

Jasper Gwyn wasn't sure he could explain it. He felt like getting up—maybe if he paced back and forth he could do it.

"I didn't know exactly what it might mean to write a portrait, and now I do. There's a way of doing it that has a meaning. Then maybe it's more successful or less, but it's a thing that exists. It's not only in my head."

"What the hell kind of trick did you come up with, can you tell me?"

"No trick, it's very simple. But in fact it doesn't occur to you until it occurs to you."

"Very clear."

"Come on, someday I'll explain it better."

"Well, tell me at least one thing."

"What do you want to know?"

"When do we give that fine studio back to John Septimus Hill and sign a nice contract?"

"Never, I think."

Tom was silent for a moment, and that wasn't a good sign.

"I found what I was looking for, Tom, it's good news."

"Not for your agent!"

"I'll never write any more books, Tom, and you're not my agent, you're my friend, and I also think you're the only one, actually."

"Am I supposed to burst into tears?"

He felt that he was irritated, but he didn't say it maliciously, it was only embarrassment or something like that. Am I supposed to burst into tears?

"Come on, Tom."

Tom was thinking that this time he couldn't straighten things out.

"And now?" he asked.

"Now what?"

"What happens now, Jasper?"

There was a long silence. Then Jasper Gwyn said something that Tom, however, couldn't understand.

"Speak into the telephone, Jasper!"

"*I don't know exactly.*"

"Ah, I see."

"I don't know exactly."

It was true up to a certain point. He had had some ideas, even quite detailed ones. Maybe there were parts missing, but he had, stamped in his mind, a hypothesis on how to proceed.

"I imagine I'll start making portraits," he simplified.

"I can't believe it."

"I'll find clients and make their portraits."

Tom Bruce Shepperd put the receiver down on the table and backed up his wheelchair. He left his office, turned with surprising skill into the corridor, and went along it until he was in front of the open door of the room where Rebecca worked. What he had to say he shouted, without ceremony.

"Will you tell me what the fuck that man has in mind and what he wants to accomplish, and, above all, why—why he has to invent all that nonsense simply in order not to do what…"

He realized that Rebecca wasn't there.

"Fuck."

He turned around and went back to his office. He picked up the phone.

"Jasper?"

"I'm here."

Tom searched for a calm tone of voice and found it.

"I'm not letting you go," he said.

"I know."

"Is there something I can do for you?"

"Certainly, but it doesn't come to mind now."

"Take your time."

"All right."

"You know where to find me."

"You, too."

"In the Laundromat."

"For example."

They were silent for a moment.

"Jasper, do you think people who make portraits have an agent?"

"I don't have the slightest idea."

"I'll find out."

But then, for days and weeks, they didn't return to the subject, because they knew that this business of the portraits was distancing them, and so they ended up circling around it, without ever approaching the heart of the matter, fearful that doing so would inevitably drive them further apart, opening them up to a suffering that they didn't want to inherit.

43.

A couple of days after that phone call with Tom, Jasper Gwyn met Rebecca—the weather was mild, and it occurred to him to make the date in Regent's Park, on that path where, in a sense, it had begun. He had brought the folder with the seven printed pages. He sat waiting on a bench with which he had a certain familiarity.

They hadn't seen each other since that last light bulb, in the dark. Rebecca arrived, and they had to figure out what point to start over from.

"Sorry to be late. Someone committed suicide on the Underground."

"Seriously?"

"No, I was late and that's all. I'm sorry."

She was wearing fishnet stockings. You could barely see them, under the long skirt. The ankles, and that was all. But they were fishnet. Jasper Gwyn also noticed rather spectacular earrings. She didn't wear things like that when she handed over cell phones in Laundromats.

"Do you like Klarisa Rode?" he asked, pointing to the book that Rebecca was holding.

"Tremendously. It's Tom who told me about her. She must have been an extraordinary woman. You know that none of her books were published while she was alive? She didn't want them to be."

"Yes, I know."

"And for at least seventy years nothing more was known about them. They were rediscovered only about ten years ago. Have you read them?"

Jasper Gwyn hesitated a moment.

"No."

"Too bad. You should."

"You've read them all?"

"Well, there are just two. But, you know, in these cases stuff continues to come out of the drawers for years, so I'm confident."

They laughed.

Jasper Gwyn kept staring at the book so Rebecca asked him, joking, if he had invited her there to talk about books.

"No, no, sorry," said Jasper Gwyn.

He seemed to chase something out of his thoughts.

"I asked to see you because I had this to give you," he said.

He took the folder and gave it to her.

"It's your portrait," he said.

She made a move as if to take it, but Jasper Gwyn held on to it because he wanted to add something.

"Would you do me the kindness of reading it here, in front of me? Do you think it's possible? It would be helpful to me."

Rebecca took the folder.

"I stopped saying no to you a long time ago. Can I open it?"

"Yes."

She did it slowly. She counted the pages. She ran her fingers over the first one, as if she were enjoying the texture of the paper.

"Have you let anyone else read it?"

"No."

"I counted on that, thank you."

She placed the pages on top of the closed folder.

"Shall I go ahead?" she asked.

"When you like."

Around them were children running, dogs pulling in the direction of home, and old couples with an air of having escaped something terrifying. Their lives, probably.

Rebecca read slowly, with a mild concentration that Jasper Gwyn appreciated. A single expression on her face the whole time: just the hint of a smile, unmoving. When she finished one page she slid it under the others. Hesitating just an instant, while she was reading the first lines of the next page. When she reached the end she sat for a while, with the portrait in her hands, looking up at the park. Without saying anything she went back to the pages and began to skim them, stopping here and there, re-reading. Every so often she compressed her lips, as if something had pricked her, or grazed her. She put the pages in order, finally, and returned them to the folder. She closed it with the tie. It was still resting on her knees.

"How do you do it?" she asked. Her eyes were bright with tears.

Jasper Gwyn took back the folder, but gently, as if it were under-stood that it had to be like that.

Then they talked for a long time, and Jasper Gwyn was pleased to explain more things than he would have expected. Rebecca asked, but carefully, as if she were opening something fragile—or an unex-pected letter. They talked at their own pace, and there was no longer anything else around them. Every so often, between one question and the next, came an empty silence, in which both measured how much they were willing to find out, or to explain, without losing the pleasure of a certain mystery, which they knew was indispens-able. At a question more inquisitive than the others Jasper Gwyn smiled and answered with a gesture—the palm of a hand passing over Rebecca's eyes, as when one says good night to a child.

"I'll keep it all to myself," Rebecca said at the end.

She couldn't know that it wouldn't be like that.

44.

They stayed a while longer, there, on the bench, while the park grew dim. For several days Jasper Gwyn had been pondering a particular idea and now he wondered if Rebecca would like to hear it.

"Of course," she said.

Jasper Gwyn hesitated briefly, then he said what he had in mind.

"I'll need some help, to get my new work going. And I thought that no one could help me better than you."

"Meaning?"

Jasper Gwyn explained to her that there were a lot of practical things to arrange, and he couldn't really imagine looking for clients, or choosing them, or something like that. Not to mention the price, and the ways of defining and collecting it. He said he absolutely needed someone to do all that for him.

"I know that the most logical solution would be Tom, but it's hard now for me to talk to him about it, I don't think he wants to understand. I need someone who believes in it, who knows it's all real and makes sense."

Rebecca listened, surprised.

"You want me to work for you?"

"Yes."

"For this business of the portraits?"

"Yes. You're the only person in the world who really knows what they are."

Rebecca shook her head. That man certainly liked to complicate her life. Or resolve it, who knows.

"Just a minute," she said. "A minute. Don't be in such a hurry."

She got up, left the book by Klarisa Rode to Jasper Gwyn, and headed toward a kiosk that sold ice cream, farther along the path. She got a cone with two scoops, which wasn't very easy, because she couldn't find her wallet. She returned to the bench and sat down again next to Jasper Gwyn. She held out the cone.

"Would you like a taste?" she asked.

Jasper Gwyn shook his head no, he didn't, and from far away the candies of the woman in the rain scarf came back to him.

"First I have to explain something to you," said Rebecca. "I left the house in order to explain it, and now I'll explain it to you. If you want to continue to make portraits, it will be useful to you."

She stopped a moment to lick the cone.

"In that studio everything is illogically easy, or at least it was for me. Seriously, you're in there, and there's nothing that after a moment does not become, in some sense, natural. It's all easy. Except for the end. That's the thing I wanted to tell you. If you want my opinion, the end is horrendous. I also asked myself why, and now I think I know."

She was careful not to let the ice cream drip; every so often she glanced at it.

"It might seem stupid to you, but at the end I would have expected you to at least hug me."

She said it like that, very simply.

"Maybe I would have liked to make love with you, there, in the darkness, but certainly I would have expected at least to end up in your arms, in some way, to touch you, *touch you*."

Jasper Gwyn was about to say something, but she stopped him with a wave of her hand.

"Look, don't get the wrong idea, I'm not in love with you, I don't think—it's something else, and it has to do just with that particular moment, that darkness and that moment. I don't know if I can explain it, but all those days when you are basically your body and almost nothing else... all those days set up a kind of expectation that something physical should happen, at the end. Something that rewards you. A distance that's filled in, I'd like to say. You fill it in by writing, but I? We? All the people who'll have their portraits done? You'll send them home as you sent me, at the same distance as there was the first day? Well, it's not a good idea."

She glanced at the ice cream.

"Maybe I'm wrong, but they'll all feel the same thing I felt."

She tidied up the dripping ice cream.

"Someday you'll write a portrait for an old man, and it won't make any difference, at the end that man will look for a way to touch you—against any logic or desire, he'll feel the need to touch you. He'll come over and run a hand through your hair, or shake your arm hard, even just that, but he'll have a need to do it."

She looked up at Jasper Gwyn.

"Well, let him do it. In some way you owe it to him."

She had reached the crunchy part, the cone.

"It's the best part," she noted.

Jasper Gwyn let her finish, then asked if she would work for him. But in a tone in which he might have said that he was charmed by her.

Rebecca thought that this man loved her, only he didn't know it, and would never know it.

"Of course I'll work for you," she said. "If you promise to keep your hands to yourself. I'm joking. Give me back the Rode, or do you want to keep it and read it?"

Jasper Gwyn seemed on the point of saying something, but then he simply gave her the book.

Three weeks later, in some journals carefully chosen by Rebecca, an advertisement appeared that, after many attempts and lengthy discussions, Jasper Gwyn had decided to reduce to three clear words.

Writer executes portraits.

As a reference it gave only a post-office box.

It won't work, the lady in the rain scarf would have said.

But the world is strange and the advertisement worked.

45.

The first portrait Jasper Gwyn made was for a man of sixty-three who all his life had sold antique timepieces. He had been married three times, and the last time he had had the bright idea of remarrying his first wife. He had asked her only not to speak of it ever again. Now he had stopped selling grandfather clocks and silver pocket watches, and went around with a multifunction Casio he had bought from a Pakistani on the street. He lived in Brighton, and had three children. The entire time he was in the studio, he walked, and not once, in the thirty-four days of his sojourn in David Barber's sound cloud, did he use the bed. When he was tired, he sat in an armchair. He would often start talking, but in an undertone, to himself. One of the few sentences that Jasper Gwyn understood, without, however, wanting to, went like this: "If you don't believe it you have only to go and ask him about it." On the twelfth day he asked if he could smoke, but then he realized that it wouldn't be right. Jasper Gwyn saw him change, over time: the way he carried his shoulders was different, and his hands were freer, as if someone had given them back to him. When the time came to talk, he did it with precision and pleasure, sitting on the floor next to Jasper Gwyn, his hands resting with well-feigned modesty on his sex. The questions didn't surprise him, and he answered the most difficult after reflecting for a long time, but also as if he had had the right words ready for years: *When I was a child and my mother went out in the evening, stylish, very beautiful,* he said. *When I wound the clocks, in the morning, in my shop, and every time I went to sleep, every blessed time.*

When the last light bulb went out, he was lying on the floor, and in the dark Jasper Gwyn, with some irritation, heard him crying, in a rather undignified way but without embarrassment. He went up to him and said, Thank you, Mr. Trawley. Then he helped him get up. Mr. Trawley leaned on his arm and with one hand sought Jasper Gwyn's face. Maybe he had in mind a caress; what resulted was a hug, and for the first time Jasper Gwyn felt the skin of a man against his own.

Mr. Trawley got his portrait in exchange for fifteen thousand pounds and a declaration in which he pledged the most absolute discretion, on the pain of heavy pecuniary sanctions. At home, while his wife was out, he turned out all the lights but one, opened the folder, and slowly read the six pages that Jasper Gwyn had prepared for him. The next day he sent a letter in which he thanked him and said that he was fully satisfied. The last line said, "I can't not think that if all this had happened many years ago I would be today a different and, in many respects, better man. Sincerely yours, Mr. Andrew Trawley."

46.

The second portrait Jasper Gwyn made was for a woman of forty, single, who after studying architecture was now occupied with an import-export business with India. Fabrics, handicrafts, occasionally the work of an artist. She lived with an Italian woman, in a loft on the outskirts of London. Jasper Gwyn made an effort to convince her that it wasn't suitable to keep her cell phone on and to arrive late every day. She learned quickly, and without apparent irritation. It was evident that she very much liked being naked and being looked at. She was thin, as if her body had been consumed by some unmet expectation, and had dark skin that had bright, animal highlights. She was loaded with bracelets, necklaces, rings, which she never took off and which she changed every day. After ten days Jasper Gwyn asked if she could come without all that junk on (he didn't describe it in those terms) and she said she would try. The next day she was completely naked, with the exception of a silver ankle bracelet. When it came time to talk she couldn't do it without pacing back and forth, and gesticulating as if words were always imprecise and needed an apparatus of physical footnotes. Jasper Gwyn ventured to ask her if she had ever been in love with a woman and she said Never but then she added, Do you want the truth? Jasper Gwyn said that there was rarely one truth.

When the last light bulb went out, she was staring at it, hypnotized. In the darkness Jasper Gwyn heard her laughing, nervously. Thank you, Miss Croner, you were perfect, he said. She got dressed, she had just a light dress, that day, and a small purse. She took out a brush and smoothed her hair, which she knew was nice and she wore long. Then, in the afternoon light that filtered faintly through the shutters, she went up to Jasper Gwyn and said it had been an incomprehensible experience. She was so close that Jasper Gwyn could have done what for days he had longed to do, but just out of curiosity—touch those highlights on her skin. He was convincing himself that he shouldn't when she kissed him on the lips, rapidly, and went off.

Miss Croner got her portrait in exchange for fifteen thousand pounds and a declaration in which she pledged the most absolute discretion, on the pain of heavy pecuniary sanctions. When she received the portrait she kept it on the table for a few days. To read it, she waited for a morning when, waking up, she felt like a queen. There were some, from time to time. The next day she telephoned Rebecca and did so repeatedly in the following days, until she was convinced that it really wasn't possible to see Jasper Gwyn again and discuss it with him. No, even just an aperitif, like two old friends, was out of the question. Then she took a sheet of her writing paper (rice paper, amber-colored) and wrote a few lines straight off. The last said, "I envy you your talent, master, your rigor, those beautiful hands, and your secretary, who is truly charming. Yours, Elizabeth Croner."

47.

The third portrait Jasper Gwyn did was for a woman who was about to be fifty and had asked her husband for a gift that could amaze her. She hadn't seen the advertisement, she hadn't dealt with Rebecca, she hadn't chosen to do what she was doing. When she arrived, the first day, she appeared skeptical, and didn't want to undress completely. She kept her slip on, of purple silk. As a young woman she had been a stewardess, because she needed to support herself and to put as many miles as possible between herself and her family. She had met her husband on the London–Dublin route. He was sitting in seat 19D and was then eleven years older than she was. Now, as often happens, they were the same age. Starting on the third day she took off her slip, and a few days later Jasper Gwyn became, without knowing it, the sixth man who had seen her completely naked. One afternoon Jasper Gwyn had all the shutters open when she arrived, and she had a moment of hesitation. But then she seemed to get used to it, and in time she came to like lingering at the windows, without covering herself, touching the glass with her breasts, which were white and beautiful. One day a boy crossed the courtyard to get a bicycle: she smiled at him. A few days later Jasper Gwyn closed the shutters again, and in some way, from that moment, she surrendered to the portrait—a different face, and another body. When the time came to talk she spoke in a girl's voice, and asked Jasper Gwyn to sit beside her. Every question seemed to catch her unprepared, but every answer was unusually acute. They talked about storms, about revenge, and about expectations. She said, at one point, that she would have liked a world without numbers, and a life without repetitions.

When the last light bulb went out, she was walking, slowly, singing in an undertone. In the darkness Jasper Gwyn watched her continue slowly, grazing the walls. He waited until she was near him and said, Thank you, Mrs. Harper, it was all perfect. She stopped and in her girlish voice asked if she could make a request. Try, Jasper Gwyn answered. I would like you to help me get dressed, she said. With tenderness, she added. Jasper Gwyn did it. It's the first time someone has done this for me, she said.

Mrs. Harper got her portrait in exchange for eighteen thousand pounds and a declaration in which she pledged the most absolute discretion, on the pain of heavy pecuniary sanctions. Her husband gave it to her on the evening of her birthday, the table set for just the two of them, by candlelight. He had wrapped the folder in gold paper and a blue ribbon. She opened the present and, sitting at the table, without saying anything, read straight through the four pages that Jasper Gwyn had written for her. When she finished, she looked up at her husband and for a moment thought that nothing could keep them from dying together, after living together forever. The next day Rebecca received an e-mail in which Mr. and Mrs. Harper thanked her for the splendid opportunity and begged her to tell Mr. Gwyn that they would jealously guard the portrait, and would never show it to anyone, because it had become the most precious thing it had been granted them to possess. Sincerely, Ann and Godfried Harper.

48.

The fourth portrait Jasper Gwyn did was of a thirty-two-year-old man who, after studying economics with excellent grades, had gotten stuck five exams from a degree, and now was a painter, with some success. His parents—members of the London upper-middle class—had not welcomed this. Until some years earlier he had been a good swimmer, and now he had a body without definition, as if reflected in a spoon. He moved slowly and yet without confidence, so you had the impression that he lived in a place stuffed with very fragile objects that only he could perceive. Even the light in his paintings—industrial landscapes—seemed to be something that only he was aware of. He had been thinking for some time of trying portraits, especially of children, and when he was close to understanding what truly interested him he had chanced to come across Jasper Gwyn's advertisement. It had seemed to him a sign. In fact what he expected was a meeting where it would be possible, at length and in the tranquility of a studio, to talk about the meaning of making a portrait of a living person, so in the first days he was dismayed by the silence that Jasper Gwyn, firmly, claimed from him and preserved in himself. He had just begun to get used to it, and to appreciate the strain, to the point of considering that it might be a rule to adopt, when something happened that to him seemed normal but in fact wasn't. It was perhaps an hour before eight, and someone knocked at the door. He saw that Jasper Gwyn gave no sign that he was aware of it. But outside the knocking began again, and continued with annoying insistence. So Jasper Gwyn got up—he was sitting on the floor, leaning against the wall, in a corner that seemed to be his den—and with an expression of infinite disbelief on his face went to the door and opened it.

There was that twenty-year-old kid, and he was holding a cell phone in his hand.

"It's for you," he said.

Jasper Gwyn was bare-chested, wearing his usual mechanic's pants. He couldn't belive it. He took the phone.

"Tom, are you mad?"

But Tom's voice wasn't there on the other end. He heard only a person weeping, very faintly.

"Hello!"

Still that weeping.

"Tom, what the fuck kind of joke is it, will you stop it?"

Then from that faint weeping the voice of Lottie emerged to tell him that Tom was ill. He was in the hospital.

"In the hospital?"

Lottie said that he wasn't well at all, then she began to weep, and finally she said could he please hurry there right away, she was asking him, please. Then she said the name of the hospital and the address, because she was a practical woman, she had always been.

"Wait," said Jasper Gwyn.

He went back into the studio to get his pad.

"Could you repeat it?" he asked.

Lottie repeated the name and address, and Jasper Gwyn wrote them on one of those cream-colored sheets. While he watched the blue ink fix on the paper the horror of a hospital name and the sterile prose of an address, he reminded himself that every spell is unspeakably fragile, and life is very swift to plunder.

He told the young man that he had to stop. Suddenly he saw him infinitely naked—and in a grotesquely useless way.

49.

Since human nature is surprisingly petty, in the taxi Jasper Gwyn thought mainly of how many people he would have to see at the hospital—colleagues, editors, journalists, quite a few extremely tiresome encounters were to be expected. He imagined the moment when they would ask what he was doing. Horrible, he thought. But when he reached the ward, only Lottie came to meet him, in the deserted corridor.

"He doesn't want anyone, he doesn't want to be seen like this," she said. "He asked only for you, a thousand times, luckily you've come, he's just asking for you."

Jasper Gwyn didn't answer, because he was looking at her, disconcerted. She was wearing spike heels and a breathtakingly short skirt.

"I know," she said. "It's Tom who asked me to. He says it keeps him in a good mood."

Jasper Gwyn nodded. Her décolletage was also of the type that keeps one in a good mood.

"He gets mad if I cry," Lottie added. "Do you mind staying here for a while? I'm dying to go somewhere and have a good cry."

In the room, Tom Bruce Shepperd was lying amid tubes and machines, as if shrunk, under sheets and blankets of a nonexistent color—hospital color. Jasper Gwyn sat down in a chair beside the bed. Tom opened his eyes. Disgusting, he said, but softly. His lips were dry and there was no light in his gaze. But then he turned a little and recognized Jasper Gwyn, and then it was different.

Softly, and slowly, they began to talk. Tom had to recount what had happened to him. His heart, somewhere. A complicated business. They'll try an operation in two days, he said. But *try* isn't much as a verb, he pointed out.

"You'll come out of it," said Jasper Gwyn. "Like the other time, you'll come out of it flying."

"Maybe."

"What do you mean *maybe*?"

"I think I'd prefer to change the subject."

"Okay."

"See if you can say something that doesn't depress me."

"That outfit of Lottie's was something."

"A pig as usual."

"I? You're the pig, you're the one who wants her to dress like that."

Tom smiled—for the first time. Then he closed his eyes again. It was evident that speaking tired him. Jasper Gwyn ran a hand through his hair, and for a moment they stayed like that, simply together.

But then, without opening his eyes, Tom said to Jasper Gwyn that he had wanted him to come for a particular reason, even though he'd give anything in the world not to be seen by him in that nauseating state. He caught his breath, and then he said it was about that business of the portraits.

"I don't want to go without knowing what the fuck you've invented," he said.

Jasper Gwyn shifted his chair a little closer to Tom's head.

"You're not going anywhere," he said.

"Just a manner of speaking."

"Try repeating it and I'll sell my whole backlist to Andrew Wylie."

"He wouldn't take you."

"That's what you say."

"Okay, but now listen to me."

Every so often he stopped to catch his breath. Or a thread he'd lost, damn.

"I've thought about it, that business of the portraits… well, I don't want to listen to a lot of nonsense. I had a better idea."

He took Jasper Gwyn's hand.

"Do it."

"What?"

"Make me a portrait, and I'll understand."

"A portrait *of you*?"

"Yes."

"Now?"

"Here. You have two days. Don't try to con me with all that nonsense that you need a month, and the studio, and the music…"

He gripped Jasper Gwyn's hand hard. It was an irrational force, no one could have said where it came from.

"Just do it. If you know how to do it, you can do it even here."

Jasper Gwyn thought of a lot of objections, all sensible. He understood with absolute lucidity that it was a grotesque situation, and regretted not having explained everything at the right moment, which was a long time ago, and certainly not now, in this hospital room.

"It's not possible, Tom."

"Why?"

"Because it's not a magic trick. It's like crossing a desert, or climbing a mountain. You can't do it in a living room just because a child you love asks you to. Let's do this: they operate, everything will go wonderfully, and when you get home I'll explain everything, I swear."

Tom let go his grip and for a moment he was silent. His breathing was a little labored now.

"It's not just that," he said finally.

Jasper Gwyn had to lean over slightly in order to hear him.

"It's important to me to understand what the hell you're up to, but it's not just that."

He clasped Jasper Gwyn's hand tightly again.

"Once you told me that making someone's portrait is a way of bringing him home. That's right?"

"Yes, something like that."

"A way of bringing him back home."

"Yes."

Tom cleared his throat. He wanted what he was about to say to be understood clearly.

"Take me home, Jasper."

He cleared his throat again.

"I don't have much time and I need to go home," he said.

Jasper Gwyn looked up because he didn't want to look into Tom's eyes.

There were all those machines, and the color of the walls, and the timbre of the hospital everywhere. He thought it was all ridiculous.

"It will be awful," he said.

Tom Bruce Shepperd relaxed his grip and closed his eyes.

"Anyway, of course you don't think I'm going to pay you," he said.

50.

So for two days and two nights, Jasper Gwyn stayed in the hospital, almost without sleeping, because he had to make a portrait of the only friend who remained to him in life. He settled himself in a corner, on a chair, and he saw doctors and nurses passing by without seeing them. He lived on coffee and sandwiches, every so often he stretched his legs in the corridor. Lottie came and didn't dare to say anything.

In his bed, Tom seemed to become smaller every day, and the silence in which he was surviving was like a mysterious disappearance. Every so often he turned toward the corner where he expected to see Jasper Gwyn and he always seemed relieved to find that it wasn't empty. When they took him away to do some test or other, Jasper Gwyn stared at the unmade bed and in that mess of sheets he seemed to see a form of nudity so extreme that it no longer needed a body.

He worked by weaving together memories and what he could now see in Tom that he had never seen. Not for a moment did it cease to be a difficult and painful activity. Nothing was like the studio, in the embrace of David Barber's music, and every rule he had established there was impossible. He didn't have his pieces of paper, he missed the Catherine de Médicis, and it was hard to think amid all those objects that he hadn't chosen. The time was insufficient, the moments of solitude rare. Noteworthy was the possibility of failure.

Yet the evening before the operation, around eleven, Jasper Gwyn asked if there was a computer, in the ward, where he could write something. He ended up in an administrative office, where they gave him a desk and the password for the employee's PC. It wasn't a normal procedure and they kept emphasizing it. On the desk were two framed photographs and a sad collection of windup mice. Jasper Gwyn adjusted the chair, which was annoyingly high. He saw with disgust that the keyboard was dirty, and intolerably so on the most frequently used keys. He would have thought the opposite should happen. He got up, turned off the overhead light, and returned to the mice. He turned on the desk lamp. He began to write.

Five hours later he got up and tried to figure out where the hell the printer was, which, he heard very clearly, was spitting out his portrait. It's odd where people put the printer in offices where there's only one printer for everyone. He had to turn on the overhead light to find it, and he discovered that he had nine pages, printed in a font he didn't especially like, paginated with margins of an offensive banality. Everything was wrong, but also everything was as it should be—a hasty precision, in which the luxury of details was removed. He didn't re-read, he merely numbered the pages. He had printed two copies: he folded one in four, put it in his pocket, and with the other in his hand he went to Tom's room.

It must have been four in the morning, he didn't even check. In the room there was only a single, fairly warm light, at the head of the bed. Tom was sleeping with his head turned to one side. The machines connected to him every so often communicated something and did it by emitting small, hateful sounds. Jasper Gwyn brought a chair to the bed. It made no sense, but he placed a hand on Tom's shoulder and began to shake him. It wasn't the kind of thing that would please a passing nurse, he realized. He brought his mouth to Tom's ear and uttered his name a few times. Tom opened his eyes.

"I wasn't sleeping," he said. "I was only waiting. What time is it?"

"I don't know. Late."

"Did you do it?"

Jasper Gwyn held the nine sheets in his hand. He placed them on the bed.

"It came out a little long," he said. "When you're in a hurry it always comes out a little long, you know."

They talked softly and had the air of boys who are stealing something.

Tom held the sheets of paper in his hand and glanced at them. Maybe he read the first lines. He had raised his head off the pillow, with the appearance of making a tremendous effort. But in his eyes there was something alert that no one had ever seen, in that hospital. He let his head fall back on the pillow and extended the pages to Jasper Gwyn.

"Okay. Read."

"Me?"

"Do I have to call the nurse?"

Jasper Gwyn had imagined something different. Like Tom reading it while he went home, finally, to take a shower. He was always a little late to admit the bare reality of things.

He took the pages. He hated reading things he had written out loud—reading them *to others*. It had always seemed to him a shameless act. But he began to do it, trying to do it well—with the necessary slowness and care. Many sentences seemed to him imprecise, but he forced himself to read everything just as he had written it. Every so often Tom chuckled. Once he made a gesture to stop him. Then he let him understand that he could continue. Jasper Gwyn read the last page even more slowly, and to tell the truth it seemed to him perfect.

At the end, he arranged the pages, folded them in two, and placed them on the bed.

The machines continued to emit inscrutable messages, with a vaguely military obtuseness.

"Come here," said Tom.

Jasper Gwyn bent over him. Now they were really close. Tom pulled an arm out from under the covers and rested one hand on his friend's head. On the nape. Then he hugged him—he leaned his friend's head against his shoulder and held it there. He moved his fingers slightly, as if to be sure of something.

"I knew," he said.

He pressed his fingers lightly on his friend's neck.

Jasper Gwyn left when Tom fell asleep. One hand was lying on the portrait, and to Jasper Gwyn it looked like the hand of a child.

51.

Rebecca was in the office when the news arrived that Tom hadn't made it. She got up and without even taking her things went out to the street. She walked quickly, as she never did, sure of what street to take and oblivious of everything around her. She arrived at Jasper Gwyn's house and rang the bell. Her desire for that door to open was so persistent that the door, finally, opened. Rebecca said nothing but threw herself into Jasper Gwyn's arms, the only place in the world where, she had decided, it would be right to cry and not stop for hours.

As often happens, it took a while to remember that, when someone dies, it's incumbent on others to live for him, too—there's nothing else appropriate.

52.

So the fourth portrait Jasper Gwyn did was of the only friend he had, a few hours before he died.

Then it was hard to start again, for many predictable reasons, but also because of the unexpected sensation that making those portraits had also been a way of challenging a person who wasn't there anymore, and through whom, probably, he had been persuaded to challenge that whole world of books he wanted to escape. Now he had no one to convince except himself, and the privacy in which he had always imagined his career as a copyist had become a sort of secret battle, almost without witnesses. He began to get somewhat accustomed to the idea that it was so, and to regain the clarity of a necessary desire. He had to go back to remember the purity of what he was looking for, and the cleanness he wished for, in the heart of his own talent. He did it calmly, letting the joy he knew re-emerge by itself—the desire. Then, gradually, he went back to work.

The fifth portrait was the one he had to do of the boy who painted, and he didn't like it at all because he had to start again from the beginning—a thing objectively doomed to failure. The sixth he did for a forty-two-year-old actor with a very strange body, like a bird's, and a memorable face, as if carved out of wood. The seventh was two very rich young people who had just married and insisted on posing together. The eighth he did for a doctor who for six months a year sailed on merchant ships, all around the world. The ninth was a woman who wanted to forget everything, except herself and four poems of Verlaine—in French. The tenth was a tailor who had dressed the Queen, without being especially proud of it. The eleventh was a girl—and that was the mistake.

Rebecca, who in choosing the candidates tried to protect Jasper Gwyn from unsuitable subjects, had in fact never met her. But there was a reason: the father had come to her, and he was not just anyone but Mr. Trawley, the retired antiques dealer, the first man in the world who had agreed to spend money to have a portrait made by Jasper Gwyn. The girl was his youngest daughter, her name was Audrey. With the courtesy and civility that Rebecca recalled appreciating when she met him, Mr. Trawley had explained that his daughter was a difficult girl and he was convinced that a singular experience like the one he had had in Jasper Gwyn's studio would perhaps help her find a truce—he said it exactly like that—where she could regain some serenity. He added that whatever Jasper Gwyn wrote in her portrait would provide for his daughter a path clearer than any reflection in the mirror and more persuasive than any lesson.

Rebecca discussed it with Jasper Gwyn and together they decided that he could do it. The girl was nineteen. She came into the studio on a Monday in May. Sixteen months had passed since he had done her father.

53.

Her nakedness was like a challenge—her young body a weapon. She talked often, and although Jasper Gwyn showed no sign of answering and was repeatedly driven to explain to her that silence was indispensable to the success of the portrait, every day she started talking again. She wasn't recounting anything, she wasn't trying to describe something: she chanted a perpetual hatred, and an indiscriminate cruelty. She was magnificent, not at all childish, and powerfully animal. For days she insulted, in a ferocious yet graceful way, her parents. Then she digressed briefly on school and her friends, but it was clear that she did it hastily, imprecisely, because she was aiming at something else. Jasper Gwyn had given up silencing her, and had grown used to considering her voice a detail of her body, only more intimate than others and in some way more dangerous—a claw. He didn't pay attention to what she said, but that caustic singsong became so vivid and seductive that it made David Barber's sound cloud seem vaguely useless, if not actually irritating. On the twelfth day the girl reached the point she had been aiming at, that is, him. She began to attack him, verbally, flare-ups alternating with silences in which she merely stared at him with unbearable intensity. Jasper Gwyn became incapable of working, and as his thoughts spun vainly he reached the point of understanding that there was something tremendously perverse and seductive in that aggression. He wasn't sure he could defend himself against it. He withstood it for two days, and on the third he didn't show up at the studio. Nor did he for the four days that followed. He returned on the fifth day, almost sure he wouldn't find her, and strangely disturbed by the idea of not being wrong. But she was there. She was silent the whole time. Jasper Gwyn felt, for the first time, that she had a dangerous beauty. He began working again, but with a troubling confusion in his head.

That evening, at home, he got a phone call from Rebecca. Something unpleasant had happened. In an afternoon tabloid, there had appeared, without specific proof but in the usual vulgar tone, a curious story about a writer who made portraits, in a studio behind

Marylebone High Street. It left out his name, but it mentioned the cost of the portraits (slightly inflated), and there were many details about the studio. There was a malicious paragraph about the nudity of the models and another that described incense, soft lighting, and new age music. According to the tabloid, having a portrait done in that manner had become, in a certain high London society, the fashion of the moment.

Jasper Gwyn had always feared something like this. But over time he and Rebecca had understood that the way of working in that studio led people to become extremely jealous of their own portraits and instinctively inclined not to damage the beauty of the experience with something that invaded the private sphere of their memory. They talked about it a little, but of all the people who had been in the studio, they couldn't think of one who would have taken the trouble to contact a tabloid and cause that mess. It was inevitable, finally, to think of the girl. Jasper Gwyn hadn't said anything about what was happening with her in the studio, but Rebecca by now could read every little detail and it hadn't escaped her that something wasn't working as usual. She tried to ask questions and Jasper Gwyn confined himself to remarking that the girl had a very special talent for spite. He wouldn't add anything else. They decided that Rebecca would monitor how the rumor circulated in the media and that for the moment the only thing to do was go back to work.

Jasper Gwyn returned to the studio the next day with the vague impression of being a lion tamer entering a cage. He found the girl sitting on the floor, in the corner where he usually squatted. She was writing something on the cream-colored pages of his notebook.

54.

Nothing much came of that story in the other papers, and Rebecca looked for Jasper Gwyn to reassure him, but she couldn't find him. He showed up after a few days, and had little to say, only that everything was fine. Rebecca knew him well enough not to insist. She stopped looking for him. She cut out the articles, just a few, from papers that had picked up the story. She said to herself that all in all it had gone well. She worked in a tiny office that Jasper Gwyn had found for her, a pleasant cubby, not far from his house. She met with three candidates (all three had read the tabloid) but none of them truly convinced her. A week passed, she waited for what always happened when the inscrutable will of the Catherine de Médicis decided that the time was up. In a few days Jasper Gwyn would deliver to her a copy of the portrait. She would then summon the client, who would come to get it, settle the bill, and give back the key to the studio. It was all habitual and repetitive, and she liked that. Only this time Jasper Gwyn was late in showing up, and instead one morning Mr. Trawley appeared. He had to say that, according to his daughter the Catherine de Médicis had gone out, and had done so in a rather elegant fashion, but the truth was that when that happened Jasper Gwyn had not been to the studio for nine days. His daughter hadn't failed to go there every afternoon, but she hadn't seen him. Now Mr. Trawley wondered if he should do something particular or just wait. He wasn't worried, but he had preferred to come in person to determine whether everything had gone well.

"Are you sure that Mr. Gwyn didn't show up for nine days?" Rebecca asked.

"My daughter says so."

Rebecca stared at him in a questioning manner.

"Yes, I know," he said. "But in this case I'm inclined to believe her."

Rebecca said that she would check and would be in touch as soon as possible. She was uneasy, but she didn't let him see it.

Before leaving, Mr. Trawley managed to ask if by any chance Rebecca had an idea of how it had gone in the studio. What he wanted to ask in reality was if his daughter had behaved decently.

"I don't know," said Rebecca. "Mr. Gwyn doesn't talk much about what happens there, it's not his style."

"I understand."

"What I guessed is that your daughter isn't an easy subject, so to speak."

"No, she isn't," said Mr. Trawley.

He paused.

"At times she can be extremely unpleasant, or excessively attractive," he added.

Rebecca thought that she would like to be a girl of whom something like that could be said.

"I'll let you know, Mr. Trawley. I'm sure that everything will be all right."

Mr. Trawley said he didn't doubt it.

The next day a long article about the portraits appeared in the *Guardian*. It was more detailed that the one in the tabloid and went so far as to mention the name of Jasper Gwyn. There was also a second small article about him, with an account of his career.

Rebecca hurried to look for Jasper Gwyn. She didn't find him at home, nor was a tour of the neighborhood Laundromats of any use. He seemed to have disappeared.

55.

Nothing happened for five days. Then Rebecca received from Jasper Gwyn a thick envelope containing the portrait of the girl, wrapped with the usual meticulous care, and a note of a few lines. He said that it would be impossible for him to be in touch for a while. He counted on the fact that in the meantime Rebecca would look after everything. He would have to delay the next portrait: he wasn't sure he could return to work for a couple of months. He thanked her and signed off with a big hug. He made no reference to the article in the *Guardian*.

For the entire day Rebecca had to politely refuse the many telephone calls that, from all over, arrived from people wanting to know more about the story of Jasper Gwyn. She didn't like being left alone at such a delicate moment, but on the other hand she knew Jasper Gwyn well enough to recognize a behavior that it would be useless to try to correct. She did what she had to do, as well as she could, and before evening she telephoned Mr. Trawley to tell him that the portrait was ready. Then she unplugged the phone, took the girl's portrait, and opened it. It was a thing that she never did. She had made it a rule to hand over the portraits without even glancing at them. It would have been the right moment to read them, she had always thought. But that evening everything was different. There was in the air something that resembled the breaking of a spell, and suspending the usual actions seemed to her reasonable, maybe even right. So she opened the portrait of the girl and began to read it.

It was four pages. She stopped at the first, then put the pages back in order and closed the folder.

56.

The girl arrived in the morning, by herself. She sat down facing Rebecca. She had long blond hair, straight and fine, that hung down on the sides of her face. Only at times, with a movement of her head, did she fully reveal her features, which were angular but dominated by two enchanting dark eyes. She was thin, and she displayed her own body with no signs of nervousness: she seemed to have chosen a kind of refined stillness as a rule of her being. She wore a jacket open over a purple T-shirt through which her small, shapely breasts could be imagined. Rebecca noticed her hands, which were pale and covered by tiny wounds.

"Your portrait," she said, handing her the folder.

The girl left it on the table.

"Are you Rebecca?" she asked.

"Yes."

"Jasper Gwyn talks about you a lot."

"It's hard for me to believe that. Mr. Gwyn isn't the type to talk much about something."

"Yes, but about you he does."

Rebecca made a vague gesture and smiled.

"Well," she said.

Then she handed the girl a piece of paper to sign. To settle the bill she had made an arrangement with the father.

The girl signed without reading it. She gave back the pen. She gestured toward the portrait.

"Did you read it?"

"No," Rebecca lied. "I never do."

"How stupid."

"What?"

"I would."

"You know, I'm old enough to decide myself what's best to do and what isn't."

"Yes, you're grown-up. You're old."

"It's possible. Now I have a lot to do, if you don't mind."

"Jasper Gwyn says that you're a very unhappy woman."

Then Rebecca looked at her for the first time unwarily. She saw that she had an odious way of being charming.

"Even Mr. Gwyn is wrong every so often," she said.

The girl made the movement with her head that revealed her face for a moment.

"Are you in love with him?"

Rebecca looked at her and didn't answer.

"No, that wasn't the question I wanted to ask," the girl corrected herself. "Have you made love with him?"

Rebecca thought of getting up and showing the girl to the door. It was obviously the only thing to do. But she also felt that if there was a way of penetrating the strange things that were happening, right in front of her she had the only possible path, however odious.

"No," she said. "I haven't made love with him."

"I have," said the girl. "Are you interested in knowing how he does it?"

"I'm not sure."

"Violently. But then all of a sudden tenderly. He likes to touch himself. He never speaks. He never closes his eyes. He's very handsome when he comes."

She said it without taking her gaze from Rebecca's eyes.

"Do you want to read the portrait with me?" she asked.

Rebecca shook her head no.

"I don't think I want to know anything else about you, girl."

"You don't know anything about me."

"There, perfect."

For a moment the girl seemed distracted by something she had seen on the table. Then she looked up again at Rebecca.

"We did it for two days, almost without sleeping," she said. "There in the studio. Then he left and never returned. A coward."

"If you don't have any other venom to spit out, our conversation is over."

"Yes, only one more thing."

"Hurry up."

"Would you do me a favor?"

Rebecca looked at her, dismayed. The girl again made that movement that revealed her face for a moment.

"When you see him tell him I'm sorry about that thing in the newspapers, I didn't think it would be such a mess."

"If you wanted to hurt him you've succeeded."

"No, I didn't want that. It was something else."

"What?"

"I don't know… I wanted to *touch him*, but I don't think you can understand."

Rebecca thought with irritation that she understood very well. She also thought of the sentence that condemns those—they are many—who aren't capable of touching without hurting, and instinctively her eyes sought those hands and the little wounds. She felt the shadow of a distant compassion and understood immediately what had subdued Jasper Gwyn, in the studio, with that girl.

"The key," she said.

The girl looked in her purse and placed the key on the table. She looked at her for a moment.

"I don't want the portrait," she said. "Throw it away."

She left the door open behind her—she walked at a slight angle, as if she had to fit into a narrow space and were doing so in order to flee everything in existence.

57.

It took Rebecca some time to recover her thoughts. She ignored the duties that she should have performed, she cancelled all her appointments, she left on the table, without opening them, the newspapers she had bought. It annoyed her to see that her hands were trembling—it was even hard to know if it was rage or some form of fear. The telephone rang and she didn't answer. She picked up her things and left.

On the way home, she sat down in a tranquil place, on the steps of a church, at the edge of a small garden, and forced herself to remember the girl's words. She tried to understand what, each time, they had shattered. Many things: some that she knew were delicate but also solid, the way simple illusions are not. Oddly, she thought of Jasper Gwyn before she thought of herself, like someone who, getting up from a fall, checks to be sure that his glasses aren't smashed, or his watch—the most fragile things. It was an effort to figure out how much that girl had wounded him. Certainly she had violated a boundary that up to that moment Jasper Gwyn had chosen as an unbreakable rule of his curious work. But it was also possible that so much attention given to placing limits and restrictions concealed in him the inner desire to go beyond every rule, even just once, and at whatever price—as if to get to the end of a particular path. Therefore it was hard to say if the girl had been a mortal blow or the end toward which all his portraits had been directed. Who knows. Certainly those nine days without setting foot in the studio made one think of a man who was frightened rather than of one who had arrived—and the fact that he remained hidden, calm but determined. Wounded animals move like that. She thought of the studio, of the eighteen Catherine de Médicis, of the music of David Barber. What a pity, she said to herself. What an immense pity if it should all end here.

She went home, walking slowly, and only then did it occur to her to think of herself, to check her own wounds. Although it disgusted her to admit it, that girl had taught her something that was humiliating, and that had to do with courage, or shamelessness, who knows. She tried to remember the moments when she, too, had been truly close to Jasper Gwyn, outrageously close, and in the end asked herself what she had done wrong at those moments, or what she hadn't understood. She went back in memory to the darkness of the studio, the last night, and recalled the nothing that remained between them, incredulous that she had been unable to span it. But even more she thought of the morning when Tom died, her running to Jasper Gwyn and what followed. She recalled their fear, and the wish to stay shut up there, together, stronger than anything else. She recalled her own movements in the kitchen, her bare feet, the telephone that rang as they went on talking, in low voices. The alcohol drunk, the old records, the book covers, confusion in the bathroom. And how easy it had been to lie beside him, and sleep. Then the difficult dawn, and the frightened gaze of Jasper Gwyn. She who understood and left.

How much more precise the sharp gesture of that girl had been. What an odious lesson.

She looked at herself and wondered if everything couldn't be explained simply by her body, unsuitable and wrong. But there was no answer. Only a sadness that for a long time she hadn't wanted to face.

At home, later, she saw in the mirror that she was beautiful—and alive.

For days, therefore, she did the only thing that seemed to her appropriate—waiting. She followed coldly the increasing number of newspaper stories that took up the odd case of Jasper Gwyn, and confined herself to filing them away, in chronological order. She answered the telephone, noting diligently all the requests and assuring callers that soon she would be able to be more useful. She wasn't afraid, she knew that she had only to wait. She did it for eleven days. Then, one morning, a large package arrived in the office, accompanied by a letter and a book.

In the package were all the portraits, each in its folder. In the

letter Jasper Gwyn explained that they were the copies he had made
for himself: he begged her to keep them in a safe place, and not to
make them public in any way. He added a detailed list of things to
do: give back the studio to John Septimus Hill, get rid of the furniture
and the fixtures, clear out the office, cancel the e-mail they had used
for work, make herself unavailable to journalists who might try to get
in touch with her. He specified that he had personally taken care of
settling all the outstanding bills, and reassured Rebecca that what she
was owed would reach her as soon as possible, including a significant
bonus. He was sure she wouldn't have any problems.

He thanked her warmly, and he was anxious to say yet again
that he could not have wished for a colleague more precise, discreet,
and pleasant. He realized that a warmer farewell might have been
hoped for in every way, but he had to confess, with regret, that he
couldn't do better.

The rest of the letter was written by hand. It said:

Perhaps I should explain to you that the distance from that girl was an
insoluble theorem: I couldn't do it without making myself ridiculous,
or without wounding her, perhaps. The first thing doesn't matter to
me, but the second would cause me infinite disappointment. Please
believe simply that it couldn't be done otherwise.

Don't worry about me, I'm not bothered by what happened and
I have in mind precisely what I have to do now.

I wish for you every happiness, you deserve it.

Forever grateful, yours,
Jasper Gwyn, copyist

Then, after the signature, there was a note of a few lines. He said that he was enclosing the last book to come from the drawers of Klarisa Rode, which had just been published. He remembered clearly how that day in the park, when he brought her the portrait, she had been carrying a novel of Rode's and had spoken of it with great enthusiasm. So it had occurred to him that in the circumstances giving her the book might be a good way of coming full circle: he hoped that reading it would give her pleasure.

Nothing else.

But can a person be made like that? Rebecca thought.

She took the book, she turned it over in her hands, then she threw it against the wall—a gesture that she would remember some years later.

It occurred to her to look on the package and she found only a generic London postmark. Where Jasper Gwyn had gone she was evidently not to know. Far—that she felt with absolute certainty. It was all over, and without that solemnity that the sunset of things should always have the right to.

She got up, she put Jasper Gwyn's letter in her appointment book, and she decided that, for the last time, she would do what he had asked. Not out of duty—out of a form of melancholy precision. She took the portraits with her when she left. She thought that not reading them would be one of the pleasures of her life. When she got home, she put them at the bottom of a closet, under some old sweaters, and this was the last act that caused her some regret—to know that no one would ever know.

It took her ten days to arrange everything. To those who asked for explanations, she gave vague answers. When John Septimus

Hill asked her to give Jasper Gwyn his respectful greetings, she explained that she had no way of doing so.

"Ah, no?"

"No, I'm sorry."

"You don't think you'll see him in a reasonable amount of time?"

"I don't imagine seeing him ever again," said Rebecca.

John Septimus Hill allowed himself a vaguely skeptical smile that Rebecca considered out of place.

58.

In the years that followed, no one had any news, apparently, of Jasper Gwyn. The gossip about that peculiar obsession with the portraits slipped quickly out of the newspapers, and his name appeared less and less frequently in the literary news. It might be cited in ephemeral charts of recent English literature, and a couple of times he was mentioned in relation to other books that seemed to take up certain of his stylistic habits. One of his novels, *Sisters*, ended up on the list of "One Hundred Books to Read Before You Die" drawn up by an authoritative literary review. His English publisher and a couple of foreign publishers tried to get in touch with him, but in the past everything had been handled by Tom, and now, with his agency closed, there seemed to be no way to talk to that man. The feeling that sooner or later he would appear, and probably with a new book, was fairly widespread. Few thought that he could have truly stopped writing.

As for Rebecca, in the space of four years she reconstructed a life, choosing to start from the beginning. She had found a job that had nothing to do with books, she had left the shit boyfriend and had gone to live just outside London. One day she had met a married man who had a wonderful way of making a mess of everything he touched. His name was Robert. In the end they fell in love, and one day the man asked her if he might perhaps leave his family and try to make another one with her. It seemed an excellent idea to Rebecca. At the age of thirty-two she became the mother of a girl to whom they gave the name Emma. She began to work less and get fatter, and she regretted neither of the two. She very seldom thought of Jasper Gwyn, and always without particular emotion. They were faint memories, like postcards sent from a previous life.

Yet one day, while she was pushing Emma in her stroller down the aisles of an enormous London bookshop, she came across a special offer on paperbacks, and at the top of a pile she saw a book by Klarisa Rode. At the moment she didn't notice the title, she simply took in the fact that she had never read it. Only at the cash register did she realize that it was, in fact, the book that four years earlier Jasper Gwyn had given her, the day when everything ended. She recalled what she had done with it. She smiled. She paid.

She began to read in the Underground, since Emma had fallen asleep in the stroller, and they had quite a few stops to go. She was really enjoying it, oblivious of all the people around, when suddenly, on page sixteen, she was dumbstruck. She read a little further, in disbelief. Then she looked up and said, aloud, "Look at this son of a bitch!"

In fact what she was reading, in Klarisa Rode's book, was her own portrait, word for word, exactly the portrait that Jasper Gwyn had made for her, years earlier.

She turned to her neighbor and in a surreal way felt bound to explain, also aloud: "He copied it, he copied it from Rode, shit!"

Her neighbor didn't seem to grasp the importance of the thing, but meanwhile something had started up in Rebecca's head—like a form of delayed common sense—and she lowered her gaze to the book again.

Just a minute, she thought.

She checked the publication date and realized that something didn't add up. Jasper Gwyn had done her portrait at least a year before that. How can someone copy a book that hasn't yet been published?

She turned again toward her neighbor, but it was evident that he couldn't be of much help.

Maybe Jasper Gwyn had read it before it was published, she thought. It was a reasonable hypothesis. She vaguely recalled that the situation with Klarisa Rode's manuscripts was intricate. Nothing more likely than that Jasper Gwyn had managed, in some way, to see them before they ended up at the publisher. It made sense. But just then, from a distance, there came back to her something that Tom had said to her, a long time before. It was the day when he was explaining to her what sort of person Jasper Gwyn was. He had told her that story of the son he hadn't acknowledged. But he had also told her something else: that there were books, at least two, written by Jasper Gwyn, that were circulating in the world, *but not under his name.*

Shit, she thought.

That's why unpublished works by that woman don't stop coming out. *He writes them.*

It was madness, but it might also be the truth.

It would change quite a few things, she said to herself. Instinctively she thought back to that day when everything ended, and saw herself throwing that stupid book against the wall. Was it possible that it wasn't a stupid book but a precious gift? She had trouble putting the pieces together. For a moment the idea crossed her mind that something important had been restored to her, something that she had been owed for a long time. She was trying to understand what, exactly, when she realized that the train was at the station where she was supposed to get out.

"Shit!"

She got up and hurried out.

It took a moment to realize that she had forgotten something.

"Emma!"

She turned while the doors were closing. She began to beat the palms of her hands against the glass and yell something, but the train was slowly pulling away.

Some people had stopped and were looking at her.

"My daughter!" cried Rebecca. "My daughter's on the train!"

It was not so simple, then, to get her back.

59.

She didn't find it necessary, later, to tell the whole story to Robert, but when it was time to go to bed Rebecca said that she absolutely had to finish reading something for work and asked him to go to sleep, she would stay out there—she wouldn't be long.

"If Emma wakes up?" he asked.

"As usual. Suffocate her with a pillow."

"Okay."

He was a sweet-natured man.

Lying on the sofa, Rebecca picked up the book by Klarisa Rode, began again from the beginning, and read it to the end. It was two in the morning when she got to the last page. The story was set in a Danish town in the eighteenth century, and was about a father and his five children. She found it beautiful. Near the beginning there was, in fact, as if inlaid, the portrait that Jasper Gwyn had made of her, but Rebecca looked in vain, in the rest of the book, for something that bore significant traces of it. Nor could she find a single page that might have been written deliberately for her. Only that kind of painting, standing in a corner, with indisputable mastery.

Things had ended so long ago with Jasper Gwyn that to try to understand, now, what that whole business meant seemed for a moment an effort that she had no desire to make. It was late, the next day she had to take Emma to her mother-in-law and then rush off to work. She thought it was better to forget about it and go to bed. But as she was turning out the lights and putting some other thing in its place, she had the strange sensation of not being there, and of refining the details of someone else's life. With a prick of dismay she realized that, in a single day, a certain distance that she had worked at for years had elegantly shifted—a curtain in a gust of wind. And from far away came a nostalgia that she thought she had defeated.

So, instead of going to bed, she did something she would never have imagined doing. She opened a closet and took out from under a pile of winter blankets the folders with the portraits. She made some coffee, sat down at the table, and began to open the folders, randomly. She began to read here and there, in no order, as she might have walked through a gallery of paintings. She didn't do it to try to understand, or to find answers. Only she enjoyed the colors, that particular light, the sure step, the traces of a certain imagination. She did it because all that was a place, and in no other place would she have wanted to be that night.

She stopped when the first light of dawn was filtering in. Her eyes were burning. She felt a sudden, heavy weariness, unavoidable. She got in bed, and Robert woke just enough to ask her, without really being aware of it, if everything was all right.

"Yes, go to sleep."

She pressed against him lightly, turning onto her side, and fell asleep.

60.

The next day when she awoke she didn't understand anything. She telephoned her office to say she had an emergency and couldn't come to work. Then she brought Emma to her mother-in-law's; she was a likable woman fatter than Rebecca who couldn't stop being grateful to her for having gotten her son out of the clutches of a woman who ate only vegetarian. Rebecca said she would be back in the afternoon and added that if she happened to be late she would let her know. She kissed Emma and went home.

In the silence of the empty rooms she picked up Rode's book again. And she forced herself to think. She hated puzzles and was aware that she didn't have the right intelligence to enjoy solving them. She wasn't even so sure she wanted to reopen a story she had thought was dead and buried. But certainly she would have liked to be sure that that book had truly been a gift for her—the loving touch she had missed in that farewell of so many years ago. Just as, undeniably, she was attracted by the possibility of uncovering, on her own, as far as she could, the infinite strangeness of Jasper Gwyn.

She sat thinking for a long time.

Then she got up, took the folders with the portraits, removed from the pile the one with her portrait, and put all the others in a large purse. She dressed and called a taxi. She was driven to the neighborhood of the British Museum, because she had decided that if there was anyone in the world who could help her, it was Doc Mallory.

61.

She had met Mallory in Tom's office. He was one of the many unlikely characters who worked there, although the word *work* didn't exactly give the idea. He was around fifty, and had a real name, but everyone called him Doc. Tom had had him around for years, and considered him absolutely indispensable. Mallory, in fact, was the man who had read everything. He had a formidable memory and seemed to have spent a couple of lifetimes looking at books and cataloguing them in his remarkable mental index. When you needed something, you went to him. Normally you found him at his desk, reading. He always wore a jacket and tie, because, he maintained, books deserve respect, all of them, even the terrible ones. You went to him to find out the exact spelling of a Russian name or to get an idea of Japanese literature in the twenties. Things like that. To see him at work was a privilege. Once one of Tom's writers had run into an accusation of plagiarism; it seemed that he had copied a scene of a brawl from an American crime novel of the fifties. Tom had torn the incriminating pages out of the book and brought them to Mallory.

"See if you can recall thirty books that have a scene of this type," he said.

A couple of hours later Mallory had appeared with a detailed list of scuffles and brawls that all seemed written by the same hand.

"Incredible!" Tom had said.

"My duty," Mallory had answered, and returned to his desk, to read a biography of Magellan.

When Tom died, he had opened, with his savings, a small bookshop near the British Museum, where he had only books that he liked. Rebecca went there from time to time, more than anything for the pleasure of saying hello and talking. But that day was different, she had something very precise to ask. When she entered the shop, even before greeting him, she turned around the sign on the door that said YES, WE ARE OPEN! On the other side it said I WILL NOT RETURN SOON.

"You intend to stay for a while, it seems to me," said Mallory from behind the counter.

"You can bet on it," said Rebecca.

62.

She placed the bag on the floor and gave him a hug. Not that she exactly loved him, but something like that. He always had the same smell, of dust and anise candies.

"You don't look like someone who's come to buy a book, Rebecca."

"No. I came to make this day unforgettable for you."

"Aha."

"Doc, do you remember Jasper Gwyn?"

"Are you kidding?"

And he started off on his complete bibliography.

"Forget that, it's something else I wanted to ask you. You remember that business of the portraits?"

Mallory began to laugh. "And who doesn't—at Tom's no one talked about anything else."

"Did you ever know anything about it?"

"You were the one who knew everything."

"Yes, but did you know anything?"

"Very little. People said that he was crazy, with that idea. But there was also a rumor that he had reached the point of selling the portraits for a hundred thousand pounds each."

"If only," said Rebecca.

"You see that you're the one who knows the story?"

"Yes, but I don't know everything. I'm missing a piece and only you can help me."

"Me?"

Rebecca leaned over, took the folders out of the purse, and placed them on the counter.

Doc Mallory had been working on some bills when she entered, so he was in shirtsleeves. He turned around, went and got his jacket, put it on, and came back to the counter.

"These are them?" he asked.

"Yes."

"May I?"

He turned the folders so that they faced him, and confined himself to delicately placing his hands on them, palms open.

"Tom would have given an arm to be able to read them," he said, with a trace of sadness.

"And you?"

Mallory looked up at her. "You know, to read them would be a privilege for me."

"Then do it, Doc, I need you to do it."

Mallory was silent for a moment. His eyes were shining.

"Why?" he asked.

"I need to know if he copied them."

"*Copied*?"

"If they were taken from other books, I don't know, something of the sort."

"Come now, it wouldn't make sense."

"A lot of things don't make sense when you're talking about Jasper Gwyn."

Mallory smiled. He knew it was true.

"Have you read them?"

"More or less."

"And have you got an idea?"

"No. But I haven't read all the books in the world."

Mallory burst out laughing.

"Mind you, I haven't read them all. Often I *skim them*," he said. Then he brought the folders a little closer.

"I think you're crazy."

"Let's take away the doubt. Read them."

He hesitated still a moment.

"It would be an enormous pleasure."

"Then read them."

"All right, I'll read them."

"No, no, you don't understand, read them now, then forget them immediately and if you so much as mention it to anyone I'll come here personally and rip out your balls."

Mallory looked at her. Rebecca smiled.

"I was joking."

"Ah."

"But not really."

Then she took off her raincoat, looked for a chair where she could sit down, and said to Mallory that he could take all the time he needed, they had the whole day.

"Don't you have something for me to read, so I don't get bored?" she asked.

Mallory made a vague gesture toward his shelves, without even looking up from the folders, which were still closed.

"Figure it out yourself, I have work to do," he said.

63.

Two hours later Mallory closed the last folder and was still for a moment. Rebecca looked up from her book as if to say something. But Mallory waved at her, to stop her. He wanted to think a little more, or he needed time to return from some very distant place.

Finally he asked Rebecca what the clients had thought of the portraits. Just out of curiosity.

"They were always very satisfied," Rebecca answered. "They recognized themselves. It was something they didn't expect, a kind of magic."

Mallory nodded.

"Yes, I can imagine."

Then he asked another question.

"You know which is the one of Tom?"

There were no names on the portraits, they could have been portraits of anyone.

"I'm not sure, but I think I recognized him."

They looked at each other.

"The one where there are only children?" ventured Mallory.

Rebecca nodded.

"I would have bet on it," Mallory said, laughing.

"It's really Tom, no?"

"Spitting image."

Rebecca smiled at him. It was incredible how that man had understood everything practically without asking a single question. Maybe reading thousands of books isn't so useless, she thought.

Then she remembered that she was there to find out something very particular.

"And the business of the copying, what do you say, Doc?"

She said it as if it were not, after all, a very important detail.

Mallory hesitated a moment. He made some vague gestures and gained time by taking out a large handkerchief and noisily blowing his nose. While he refolded it and put it in his pocket he said that he had already read one of those portraits. He took out one folder from the others and put it on the table. He opened it. He re-read some lines.

"Yes, this comes directly from another book," he said reluctantly.

Rebecca felt a sharp stab of pain somewhere and couldn't hide a grimace.

"Are you sure?"

"Yes."

Everything was becoming damnably more complicated.

"Do you remember what book it is?" she asked.

"Yes, it's titled *Three Times at Dawn*. A beautiful book, short. I remember the first part as very similar to this portrait, maybe not literally the same, I think it's longer. But some sentences I could swear are identical. And the scene is the same, the two in a hotel, there's no doubt."

Rebecca ran a hand through her hair. Fuck, she thought. She took the open folder, turned it, glanced at the beginning of the portrait. One of the finest. Damn.

"Do you have that book?" she asked.

"No, I had it but it disappeared immediately. A small publisher brought it out, in very few copies—it was a kind of oddity."

"In what sense?"

"Well, it was found among the papers of an old music teacher, an Indian who had died some years earlier. No one supposed that he had ever written anything, but that story turned up. They thought it was good and they published it—maybe a couple of years ago. But a thousand copies, even less. A trifle."

Rebecca looked up at him.

"What did you say?"

"In what sense?"

"Repeat what you said."

"Nothing… That an Indian man, now dead, wrote it some years ago, someone who did something else, who in his life had never published anything. You know, a kind of tidbit, no? But very beautiful, I have to say. The typical thing that someone like Jasper Gwyn could have read."

The typical thing that someone like Jasper Gwyn could have written, thought Rebecca. And Doc Mallory couldn't understand why she suddenly appeared on the other side of the counter, and was embracing him. Nor did he understand well those red eyes.

"Doc, I love you."

"You should have told me years ago, baby."

"He didn't copy them, Doc, he certainly didn't copy them."

"Really, I just demonstrated the opposite."

"Someday I'll explain, but you have to believe me, he didn't copy them."

"And how do you explain *Three Times at Dawn*?"

"Forget it, you can't understand, just tell me if you have it."

"I told you. No."

"You never have anything."

"Hey, Missy!"

"I'm joking, come on, write down the author and title."

Mallory did it. Rebecca glanced at it.

"Akash Narayan, *Three Times at Dawn*, okay."

"The publisher had one of those ridiculous names like Wheat and Corn. That type."

"I'll sort it out. Now I have to go and find it."

She picked up the folders, put them in her purse. While she put on her raincoat she reminded Mallory of what would happen if he merely dared to mention to someone what he had read that day.

"All right, all right."

"I'll be back soon and tell you everything. You're great, Doc."

She hurried off as if she were years late. In a certain sense she was.

Before closing that evening, Doc Mallory went to the shelf where he had two of the three novels by Jasper Gwyn (the first he had never liked). He took them down, and for a while turned them over in his hands. He said something in an undertone, inclining his head slightly, maybe in a bow.

64.

Rebecca found *Three Times at Dawn* in an enormous bookstore at Charing Cross, and for the first time thought that those odious supermarkets of books made sense. She couldn't resist the temptation, and began to leaf through it there, sitting on the floor, in a tranquil corner that displayed child-care books.

The publisher in fact had a name like that. Vine and Plow. Horrible, she thought. On the jacket flap there was a biographical note about Akash Narayan. It said he was born in Birmingham and had died there at ninety-two, having spent his life teaching music. It didn't specify what type. Then it said that *Three Times at Dawn* was his only book, and that it had been published posthumously. Nothing else. Not even a hint of a photograph.

Nor did the back cover say much. It revealed that the story took place in an unspecified English city, and that it all unfolded in a couple of hours. But a very paradoxical couple of hours, it added, in a deliberately enigmatic tone.

Glancing at the frontispiece she discovered that the book had been written in Hindi, and only afterward translated into English. The name of the translator said nothing to her. But it was, instead, with great satisfaction that she read the curious dedication that appeared at the head of the first chapter.

For Catherine de Médicis and the master of Camden Town.

"Welcome back, Mr. Gwyn," she said in a low voice.
Then she hurried home, because she had a book to read.

65.

She left Emma to sleep at her grandmother's, and asked Robert if he would go out to the movies with some friends because she absolutely had to stay home alone that night. She had a really difficult job to do and she would like to do it with no one wandering around the house. She said it in a nice way, and he, as noted, had a sweet nature. He asked only what time he could come back.

"Not before one?" Rebecca tried.

"Let's see," he said. He had had in mind an evening with half an hour of television and early to bed.

Then, before going out, he kissed her and asked only: "I shouldn't worry, right?"

"Absolutely not," said Rebecca, although she wasn't entirely sure.

Alone, she sat at the table and began to read.

Predictably, Doc wasn't wrong. *Three Times at Dawn* was in three parts, and the first was very similar to one of Jasper Gwyn's portraits. It even turned out to be true that it was a little longer, but, when she began to check, Rebecca determined that all the important things were there. Without any doubt the two texts were close relatives.

Nor was Doc wrong in saying that the book was a beautiful book. The other two parts flowed so smoothly that Rebecca ended up reading them, forgetting for long stretches the real reason that she was doing it. The book consisted mainly of dialogues, and there were two principal characters, the same ones in each part, but there was something paradoxical and surprising about it. At the end she regretted that Akash Narayan had wasted all that time as a music teacher, when he could write like this. Provided she believed that he truly existed, obviously.

Rebecca got up to make coffee. She looked at the time, and saw that she still had a good bit of the evening. She got out Jasper Gwyn's portraits and put them on the table.

All right, she said to herself. To summarize: Rode doesn't exist, it's Jasper Gwyn who writes her books. Same goes for Akash Narayan. And so far we've got it, she thought. Why he put my portrait in Klarisa Rode's book I can imagine: because he loved me (she smiled at this thought). Now let's see if we can discover why the hell he put the other portrait in *Three Times at Dawn*. And that portrait in particular. Who is this shit who deserved a gift as nice as mine? she wondered. She was beginning to enjoy herself.

The problem was that there was nothing in the portraits entrusted to her by Jasper Gwyn that could be traced back with certainty to one of the clients who had paid to have them done. Not a name, not a date, nothing. Besides, the simple but singular technique with which they had been executed made it difficult to recognize the person who had inspired them, unless you had a profound familiarity with him. In other words, it looked like an impossible job.

Rebecca began to proceed by elimination. She had read a page of the portrait of the girl, and she was gratified to be able to say that the one in *Three Times at Dawn* wasn't hers. The portrait of Tom she thought she had recognized, and if she had doubts Mallory had removed them: so that, too, could be eliminated (a pity, she thought, it was the only case that would not trouble her). So nine remained.

She took a piece of paper and listed them in a column.

Mr. Trawley
The forty-year-old with the mania about India (*Aha, she thought.*)
The former hostess
The boy who painted

The actor

The two who had just gotten married

The doctor

The woman with her four Verlaine poems

The queen's tailor

End

She set aside the folders with her portrait, Tom's, and the girl's. Then she opened the others and arranged them on the table.

And now let's see if I can get somewhere.

She tried to come up with hypotheses, and several times she moved the open folders on the table, trying to match them with the people on the list. It was head-splitting, and for that reason it was some time before Rebecca noticed a detail that she should have noticed long ago, and which left her bewildered. The characters were nine but the portraits ten.

She checked three times, but there was no doubt.

Jasper Gwyn had sent her one extra portrait.

Impossible, she thought. She had made the arrangements, one by one, for those portraits, she had followed them from the beginning to the end, and it was unthinkable that for all the time they had worked together Jasper Gwyn had managed to make one that she knew nothing about.

That portrait shouldn't have existed.

She counted again.

No, there really were ten.

Where did this tenth come from? And who the hell was it?

She understood suddenly, with the blazing speed with which

we understand, long afterward, things that have been in front of us forever, had we only known how to look.

She picked up the portrait that was in *Three Times at Dawn* and began to re-read it.

How could I not have thought of this before?, she asked herself.

The hotel lobby, shit.

She continued to read, avidly, as if swallowed by the words.

Hell, it's him, exactly, she thought.

Then she looked up and realized that all the portraits made by Jasper Gwyn would remain hidden, as he had wished, but that two would be hidden in a singular fashion, wandering through the world sewn secretly into the pages of two books. One she knew well, and it was hers. The other she had just recognized, and it was the portrait that any painter sooner or later attempts—a self-portrait. From a distance, it seemed to her, they looked at each other, a handbreadth above the others. Now yes, she thought—now it's the way I never stopped imagining it.

She got up and looked for something to do. Something simple. She began to straighten up the books that were lying around, all over the house. She merely placed them on top of one another, but in small piles, from the biggest to the smallest. Meanwhile she thought of the delayed sweetness of Jasper Gwyn, turning it over in her mind, in the pleasure of observing it from every side. She did it in the light of a strange happiness that she had never felt before, yet which she seemed to have carried with her for years, waiting. It seemed impossible that, in all that time, she could have done anything except guard it and hide it. What we are capable of, she thought. Growing up, loving, having children, growing old—and all this while we are elsewhere, in the long time of an answer that doesn't arrive, or of a gesture that doesn't end. How many paths, and at what a different pace we retrace them, in what seems a single journey.

When Robert came home, passably drunk, she was still awake, but sitting on the sofa. Scattered on the table were all those folders.

"Everything all right?" he asked.

"Yes."

"Sure?"

"Yes, I think so."

66.

Then she could have done many things, and one certainly: discover where Jasper Gwyn was hiding. It wouldn't be difficult to track him down, by going to Rode's publisher or the publisher of *Three Times at Dawn*. Surely in exchange for silence they would give her an address, or something.

Yet for several days she lived her normal life, only allowing herself from time to time some secret thoughts. Every so often she lost herself in imagining a scene of arriving in some ridiculous place, and sitting in front of a house, to wait. She imagined never returning. Many times she wrote and rewrote in her mind a short letter, handwritten, in an elegant script. She would like him to know that she knew, nothing more. And that she was delighted by it. Every so often she thought of Doc, and how wonderful it would be to tell him about it. Or how wonderful it would be to tell everything to anyone, over and over again.

While in the meantime she lived her everyday life.

When she felt that it was the moment, among all the things that she could have done she chose one, the smallest—the last.

67.

She arrived in Camden Town, and had to ask quite a few people before she found the shop of the old man with the light bulbs. She found him sitting in a corner, his hands still. Things must not be going too well.

"May I?" she asked, entering.

The old man made one of his gestures.

"My name is Rebecca. Years ago I worked with Jasper Gwyn, do you remember?"

The old man pressed a button and the shop was lighted by a soft, weary light.

"Gwyn?"

"Yes. He came here for light bulbs for his studio. He got eighteen every time, always the same ones."

"Of course I remember, I'm old, I'm not an idiot."

"I didn't mean that."

The old man got up and approached the counter.

"He doesn't come anymore," he said.

"No. He doesn't work in the city. He closed the studio. He went away."

"Where?"

Rebecca hesitated a moment.

"I don't have the slightest idea," she said.

The old man gave a hearty laugh, less old than he was. He seemed happy that Jasper Gwyn had managed to disappear without a trace.

"Sorry," he said.

"For what?"

"I have a weakness for people who disappear."

"Don't worry, so do I," said Rebecca.

Then she pulled a book out of her purse.

"I brought you something. I thought it would please you."

"Me?"

"Yes, you."

She placed *Three Times at Dawn* on the counter. It was the copy she had read, she hadn't been able to find another one.

"What is it?" the old man asked.

"A book."

"I see. But what is it?"

"A book that Jasper Gwyn wrote."

The old man didn't even touch it.

"I stopped reading six years ago."

"Really?"

"Too many light bulbs. My vision is ruined. I prefer to save it for work."

"I'm sorry. In any case, you don't really have to read the book, you just have to read one line."

"What is it, a game?" the old man asked, now a little angry.

"No, no, nothing of the sort," said Rebecca.

She opened the book to the first page and moved it toward the old man.

The old man didn't touch it. He gave Rebecca a suspicious glance, then bent over the book. He had to get really close, with his nose almost touching the paper.

There was just the title and the dedication to read. It took a while. Then he raised his head.

"What does it mean?" he asked.

"Nothing. It's a dedication. Jasper Gwyn dedicated the book to you, that's all. To you and those bulbs, it seems to me."

The old man lowered his head again in that extreme way and read it all again. He wanted to check carefully.

He got up again and took the book out of Rebecca's hands, with a care that he usually reserved for the light bulbs.

"Does it talk about me?" he asked.

"No, I really don't think so. He dedicated it to you because he admired you. I'm sure of that. He had a great respect for you."

The old man swallowed. He turned the book over in his hands for a while.

"Keep it," Rebecca said. "It's yours."

"Seriously?"

"Of course."

Smiling, the old man lowered his gaze to the book and stared at the cover.

"The name of Mr. Gwyn isn't there," he pointed out.

"Every so often Jasper Gwyn likes to write books under a pseudonym."

"Why?"

Rebecca shrugged her shoulders.

"It's a long story. Let's say he likes to make himself untraceable."

"Disappear."

"Yes, disappear."

The old man nodded, as if he were perfectly able to understand.

"He told me he was a copyist," he said.

"It wasn't completely false."

"Meaning?"

"When you knew him he was copying people. He made portraits."

"Paintings?"

"No. He *wrote* portraits."

"Is that something that exists?"

"No. That is, it began to exist when he began to do it."

The old man thought about it. Then he said that light bulbs made by hand also didn't exist before he began to make them.

"At first they all thought I was crazy," he added.

Then he said that the first person to believe in him was a countess who wanted in her living room a light exactly like the light of dawn.

"It wasn't at all easy," he recalled.

They were silent for a while, then Rebecca said that she really had to go.

"Yes, of course," said the old man. "You were too kind to come here."

"I did it happily, I was there in the light of your light bulbs. It's a light that is very difficult to forget."

There might have been tears in the old man's eyes, but it was impossible to say, because the eyes of the old are always a little weepy.

"You would honor me if you would accept a small gift," he said.

He went to a shelf, took a light bulb, wrapped it in tissue paper, and gave it to Rebecca.

"It's a Catherine de Médicis," he explained. "Treat it with care."

Rebecca took it with great attention and put it in her purse. It was as if he had given her a small animal. Alive.

"Thank you," she said. "It's a beautiful gift."

She went toward the door and just before opening it she heard the old man's voice pronouncing a question.

"How did he do it?"

She turned.

"Excuse me?"

"How did Mr. Gwyn *write* portraits?"

Rebecca had heard that question dozens of times. She began to laugh. But the old man remained serious.

"I mean, what the devil did he write in those portraits?"

Rebecca had an answer that she had practiced using for years, every time someone asked her that question, to cut it off. She was about to utter it when she felt that soft, weary light around her. So she said something else.

"He wrote stories," she said.

"Stories?"

"Yes. He wrote a piece of a story, a scene, as if it were a fragment of a book."

The old man shook his head.

"Stories aren't portraits."

"Jasper Gwyn thought so. One day, when we were sitting in a park, he explained to me that we all have a certain idea of ourselves, maybe crude, confused, but in the end we are pushed to have a certain idea of ourselves, and the truth is that often we make that idea coincide with some imaginary character in whom we recognize ourselves."

"Like?"

Rebecca thought for a moment.

"Like someone who wants to go home but can't find the way. Or someone who always sees things a moment before others do. Things like that. It's what we are able to intuit about ourselves."

"But it's idiotic."

"No. It's imprecise."

The old man stared at her. It was clear that he wanted to understand.

"Jasper Gwyn taught me that we aren't characters, we're stories," said Rebecca. "We stop at the idea of being a character engaged in who knows what adventure, even a very simple one, but what we have to understand is that we are the whole story, not just that character. We are the wood where he walks, the bad guy who cheats him, the mess around him, all the people who pass, the color of things, the sounds. Do you understand?"

"No."

"You make light bulbs, has it ever happened that you saw a light in which you recognized yourself? That was really you?"

The old man recalled a Chinese lantern above the door of a cottage, years before.

"Once," he said.

"Then you can understand. A light is just a segment of a story. If there is a light that is like you, there will also be a sound, a street corner, a man who walks, many men, or a single woman, things like that. Don't stop at the light, think of all the rest, think of a story. Can you understand that it exists, somewhere, and if you find it, that would be your portrait?"

The old man made one of his gestures. It resembled a vague yes. Rebecca smiled.

"Jasper Gwyn said that we are all a few pages of a book, but of a book that no one has ever written and that we search for in vain in the bookshelves of our mind. He told me that what he tried to do was write that book for the people who came to him. The right pages. He was sure he could do it."

The eyes of the old man smiled.

"And did he?"

"Yes."

"How did he do it?"

"He looked at them. For a long time. Until he saw in them the story they were."

"He looked at them and that's all."

"Yes. He talked a little, but not much, and only once. More than anything he let time pass over them, carrying off a lot of things, then he found the story."

"What kind of stories?"

"There was everything. A woman who tries to save her son from a death sentence. Five astronomers who live only at night. Things like that. But just a fragment, a scene. It was enough."

"And the people in the end recognized themselves."

"They recognized themselves in the things that happened, in the objects, the colors, the tone, in a certain slowness, in the light, and also in the characters, of course, but in all of them, not one, all of them, simultaneously—you know, we are a lot of things, and all at the same time."

The old man sniggered, but in a nice way, politely.

"It's hard to believe you," he said.

"I know. But I assure you it's so."

She hesitated a moment. Then she added something that she seemed to understand just at that moment.

"When he did my portrait, I read it, at the end, and there was a landscape, at one point, four lines of a landscape, and I *am* that landscape, believe me, I am that whole story, I am the sound of that story, the pace and atmosphere, and every character of that story, but with a disconcerting precision I am even that landscape, I have always been, and will be forever."

The old man smiled at her.

"I'm sure it was a very beautiful landscape."

"It was," said Rebecca.

The old man, finally, moved toward her, to say goodbye. Rebecca shook his hand and realized she was doing it cautiously, as years before she had been accustomed to do with Jasper Gwyn.

68.

Recently another book by Klarisa Rode has come out, which is unfinished. It appears that death surprised her when, according to the plans contained in her notes, she still had at least half left to write. It's a curious text because, against all logic, the missing part is the beginning. There are two chapters out of four, but they're the final ones. So for the reader it's an experience that could justly be called unusual, and yet it would be incorrect to judge it ridiculous. Not otherwise do we know our own parents, in fact, and sometimes even ourselves.

The protagonist of the book is an amateur meteorologist convinced that he can predict the weather on the basis of a statistical method all his own. We can imagine that the first part of the book, the nonexistent part, would consist of an account of the origins of this obsession, but it doesn't seem so important, after all, when you begin the part that Rode in fact wrote, where she reconstructs the years of research carried out by the protagonist: the goal he had set for himself was to determine the weather every day, in Denmark, for the past sixty-four years. To reach it he had had to put together a staggering mass of facts. Nonetheless, with persistence and patience, he had worked it out. The last part of the book reports that, on the basis of the statistics he collected, the amateur meteorologist was able to establish, for example, that on March 3 in Denmark the probability of sun was 6 percent. That of rain on July 26 was practically none.

To collect the data he needed, the amateur meteorologist used a method that is in fact one of the reasons for the book's fascination: he asked people. He had come to the conclusion that on average every human being distinctly recalls the weather on at least eight days of his life. He went around asking. Since each person connects the memory of the atmospheric weather to a particular moment of his life (his marriage, the death of his father, the first day of war), Klarisa Rode ended up constructing a striking gallery of characters, drawn with masterly skill in a few bold strokes. "A fascinating mosaic of real and vanished life," as an authoritative American critic put it.

The book ends in a remote village, where the amateur meteorologist has retreated, satisfied with the results he has obtained and only partly disappointed by the faint echo that their publication caused in the scientific community. A few pages from the end he dies, on a day of cold wind, after a starry night.

THREE
TIMES
AT
DAWN

For Catherine de Médicis and the master of Camden Town

1.

There was the hotel, with its slightly faded elegance. Probably in the past it had been able to keep certain promises of luxury and civility. It had, for example, a fine revolving door of wood, the sort of detail that always inspires reveries.

Through it a woman entered, at that odd hour of the night, apparently thinking of other things, having just gotten out of a taxi. She was wearing only a low-cut yellow evening dress, with not even a light scarf over her shoulders: this gave her the intriguing air of one to whom something has happened. There was an elegance in her movements, but she also seemed like an actress who has just left the stage, relieved of the obligation to play her part, and reverting to some more sincere version of herself. Thus she had a way of stepping, wearily, and of holding her tiny purse, as if letting go of it. She was no longer very young, but this suited her, as happens sometimes to women who have never had doubts about their own beauty.

Outside was the darkness before dawn, neither night nor morning. The lobby of the hotel was still: clean, soft, its features refined, its colors warm; silent, the space carefully arranged, the lighting indirect, the walls high, the ceiling pale, books on the tables, puffy cushions on the sofas, paintings thoughtfully framed, a piano in the corner, a few necessary signs in a deliberately chosen typeface, a grandfather clock, a barometer, a marble bust, curtains at the windows, carpets on the floor—a hint of perfume.

Since the night clerk, having placed his jacket over the back of a plain chair, was, in a small nearby room, sleeping the light sleep that he was a master of, there would have been no one to see the woman who entered the hotel if it weren't for a man sitting in an armchair in a corner of the lobby—irrational, at that time of night—who saw her, and then crossed his left leg over the right, when before it had been the right that rested on the left, for no reason. They saw each other.

It felt like rain, but then it didn't, said the woman.

Yes, it can't seem to make up its mind, said the man.

Are you waiting for someone?

I? No.

I'm so tired. Would you mind if I sit down for a moment?

Please.

Nothing to drink, I see.

I don't think they serve breakfast before seven.

Alcohol, I meant.

Ah, that. I don't know. I don't think so, at this hour.

What time is it?

Four twelve.

Seriously?

Yes.

This night is never going to end. It seems to me it began three years ago. What are you doing here?

I was about to leave. I have to go to work.

At this hour?

Yes.

How do you do it?

It's nothing, I like it.

You like it.

Yes.

Incredible.

You think so?

You seem like the first interesting person I've met this evening. Tonight. In short, that's what you are.

I don't dare think about the others.

Frightful.

Were you at a party?

I'm not sure I feel very well.

I'll call the night clerk.

No, for goodness' sake.

Maybe it would be better to lie down.

I'll take off my shoes, do you mind?

Of course not…

Tell me something, anything. If I'm distracted it will pass.

I wouldn't know what…

Tell me about your work.

It's not very fascinating as a subject…

Try.

I sell scales.

Go on.

There are a lot of things to be weighed, and it's important for them to be weighed accurately, so I have a factory that produces scales, of all types. I have eleven patents, and... I'm going to call the clerk.

No, please, he hates me.

Stay down.

If I stay down I'll throw up.

Sit up, then. That is, I mean...

Do you make money selling scales?

In my opinion you should...

Do you make money selling scales?

Not much.

Go on, don't think about me.

I really should go.

Do me a favor, keep talking for a little while. Then go.

I used to make a fairly good living, until some years ago. Now I don't know, I must have made a mistake somewhere, but I can't seem to sell anything anymore. I thought it was my salesmen, so I started going around myself, to sell, but in fact my products aren't popular anymore, maybe they're old-fashioned, I don't know, maybe they cost too much, in general they're very expensive, because everything is made by hand—you have no idea what it means to obtain absolute accuracy when you're weighing something.

Weighing what? Apples, people, what?

Everything. From scales for goldsmiths to ones for containers, we make everything.

Seriously?

That's why I have to go, today I have an important contract to negotiate, I really can't arrive late, my company is at stake, if this doesn't go right... Damn!

Shit.

I'll take you to the bathroom.

Wait, wait.

Oh, no!

Shit.

I'll go get some water.

I'm sorry, really, I'm sorry.

I'm going to get some water.

No, stay here, please.

Here, you can clean it up with this.

How embarrassing.

Don't worry, I have children.

What does that have to do with it?

Children often throw up. Mine, anyway.

Ah, I'm sorry.

So it's not a big deal to me. But now it would be better to go to your room.

I can't leave this mess here...

Then I'll call the clerk, you go up to your room. You have a room, right?

Yes.

Then go. I'll take care of this.

I'm not sure I remember the number.

The clerk will tell you.

I don't want to see the clerk, he hates me, I told you. Don't you have a room?

I?

Yes.

I just left it.

Take me there, please.

I told you that I just left it.

Well, what's the matter, did you burn it down? It must still be there, no?

Yes, but…

Do me a favor, take me up, then I'll stop bothering you.

I would have to get the key back.

Does that seem to you something so unreasonable?

No, of course not.

Do it, then, please.

If really… I mean…

You are truly kind.

All right, come on.

My shoes.

Yes, your shoes.

What floor is it on?

Second. Let's take the elevator.

I'm sorry to leave all this mess…

Don't think about it.

Now it's going a little better, you know?

Good. But you need to rest. Come…

I haven't forgotten anything?

Come.

What's this damn perfume in the elevator?

Lily of the valley and sandalwood.

How do you know?

They're my hobby. Perfumes.

Really?

Yes.

You sell scales and after dinner you fool around with perfumes?

More or less.

Do you make them?

I've tried. It's not easy. I study others'.

You ought to make them.

Here we are, we've arrived.

You're an odd type.

Maybe. This way.

You took the key, right?

Yes.

I'm sorry. I always think that everybody is incompetent, like me.

Don't worry.

But a person who makes scales isn't likely to be incompetent, right?

Improbable, let's say.

Right.

Please, come in.

What a gorgeous room!

They're all the same, to tell you the truth.

How can you be sure?

I've been coming to this hotel for sixteen years. The bathroom is over there. I'll leave the key here, I'll take care of explaining everything to the clerk. Now I really have to go.

You're going?

Yes, I'm going. You don't have a room here, right?

Excuse me?

You came in and said, "Gorgeous room," but if you actually had a room here you would know that it's just like yours. They're all the same.

Is detective work also a hobby of yours?

No. I pay attention to details. I make scales. You came into this hotel but you don't in fact have a room in this hotel.

You're going?

Yes, of course. I'd just like to be sure that…

I came in because I like hotel lobbies, at night. And this one is beautiful, did you notice? Not too much, not too little. I've come here other times, that's why the clerk hates me.

And if you hadn't met me?

I really have to go to the bathroom. Do you have a toothbrush and toothpaste?

Now it's really gotten late for me…

I know, just lend me a toothbrush, what does it cost you?

A toothbrush?

Calm down, hasn't anyone ever asked to borrow a toothbrush?

No one who has just vomited!

Oh, that.

Yes, that.

Will you give it to me or not?

Take it, also the toothpaste. Here. Don't make too much of a mess, please, if you like have a good sleep and then leave everything in order. I have to come back to this hotel. Goodbye.

Nice, walnut toothpaste.

It's not walnut.

It's written on it, walnut.

That's the brand. The flavor is in small writing, at the bottom.

Oh, well, all right. And what were you doing downstairs?

What?

What were you doing downstairs, sitting by yourself in an armchair at four in the morning? If you were in such a hurry, why were you there?

I wasn't in such a big hurry, *now* I am.

All right, anyway, you were there, what were you thinking about? Do you mind if I brush my teeth while you tell me?

I don't think I'll tell you a thing.

Why?

I don't even know you.

Oh, that.

Yes, that.

It looks like no one ever came into this bathroom. What is it, you use the towels and then fold them all very neatly? In a hotel? You know, there are people who are paid to do that.

I don't…

Do you make the bed, too?

I imagine that's my business.

All right, all right. It's good, this toothpaste. What is it, raspberry?

Currant, with a touch of anise.

Mmm… Good.

They also make it without the anise, but it loses a lot.

Inexcusable.

I didn't fold the towels. It's that I didn't use them. I didn't do anything. I couldn't sleep. I sat all night in that chair, with the light turned low. Then at four I came down to the lobby. Now I really have to go. It was a pleasure to meet you. Please leave the room before ten. Goodbye.

What the hell are you doing? Hey! Come back here! I say, does it seem right to behave with…

Don't shout, you'll wake everybody up.

Then come back here!

Let's not make a scene in the corridor, please.

Fine, let's do it in the elevator.

You're barefoot, the foam from the toothpaste is coming out of your mouth, and downstairs there's a clerk who wouldn't be happy to see you in that state.

If that's it your shoes are full of vomit.

No!

Come, I'll clean them.

Oh no, no!

Stop shouting, you'll wake everybody up.

But see if…

Come on, like a good boy. Take off those shoes. Not like that!

I have to untie them!

I'll do it, sit there. Since you were there all night, in that chair, a minute more or less…

Very witty.

Goodness, how disgusting…

Forget it, please.

I wouldn't dream of it. I threw up, I clean up. Here, done.

Where are you taking them?

A nice washing…

No, not in water!

Why? You'll see, it works.

I have to put on those shoes, will you tell me how the hell—

Would you answer?

What?

The telephone, the telephone's ringing.

Who the hell—

Answer.

But I'm not in this room, that is…

Do I have to answer?

No!

Look how clean they came out. Now a nice drying with the dryer…

Hello?… Yes, it's me… No, I didn't have an accident, I came back up to the room for a moment… Oh, that, yes… I didn't feel well… No, much better, I'm sorry about the carpet… If there's something to pay… No, I insist… I'm coming down now… No, really, I don't need anything… I'm coming down now… Yes, thank you, you're very kind… Thank you.

Who was it?

I have to go, right away.

Who was it?

The night clerk. Where are the shoes?

I hate that man.

Give me those shoes.

I wouldn't dream of it. Sit there a moment and I'll dry them.

I have to go. Now!

What manners! Take them if you want them so much.

I told the clerk that it was me, downstairs, who… Just do me a favor and don't let anyone see you leave. Damn, they're wet…

Why don't you forget it?

Yes, I'll go out barefoot, a fine idea.

I mean, why don't you forget the whole thing, the contract, the scales, everything.

What the hell are you talking about?

How old are you?

Me?

You, yes.

Forty-two.

You see, you're young enough to leave everything.

What do you mean?

Don't tell me you've never thought of it. Leaving everything and starting all over from the beginning. It wouldn't be bad, would it?

You're crazy.

But the woman said that a lot of people dream of starting over again, and she added that in that there was something moving, not *crazy*. She said that in fact almost no one, after all, really starts again from the beginning, but one has no idea how much time people spend fantasizing about doing it, and often while they're right in the middle of their troubles, and the life they would like to leave. She had once had a child and she recalled distinctly the anguish that gripped her every time she was alone with him, when he was little, and then the only thing that worked was to think seriously of leaving and starting over again. She planned where to leave him, the child, and already knew how she would do her hair and where she would go to look for a job, to start again. One thing that made her feel better immediately was to think of how she would spend the evenings then, and the nights. She would pass entire evenings eating on the couch, and others she would go out and go to bed with a man, she would do it with great confidence, then get up from the bed and take her things, without a regret. She said that by the sole fact of thinking all this something inside her dissolved and a serenity possessed her, as if she really had resolved something. She then became much sweeter with the child, and suddenly luminous, and maternal. The child realized it, he felt it, like a little animal, and in her arms his movements became slower, and his gaze curious. Everything seemed to go much better, like a charm. She added that she was seventeen at the time. While she was telling all this, the woman had taken off her evening dress, first unzipping the zipper at the back and then, shifting it slightly off her shoulders, letting it fall. Since the dress was silk, it crumpled on the floor in a shining, light bundle, from which she emerged with a tiny step, first one foot, then the other. Although she was now in underpants and bra she continued to talk, taking no notice of it, and betraying no intention other than to complete a gesture she had decided to make. She picked up the silk bundle and as she was telling how later, years later, she was in fact separated from that child, she placed it on a chair and went over to the bed. Still talking, she pulled down the red bedspread and at that the man grimaced slightly, as if he had been stung. But she paid no attention, she took a barrette out of her hair and slid between the sheets, which was the thing she had perhaps been thinking of, with great desire, from the moment she entered the room, probably to find a form of refuge, or gentleness, childlike. She unhooked the bra, threw it in a corner of the room, arranged the pillow, and then pulled up the sheet, up under her chin. She was telling what had happened to her once in a kind of placement office, and she still couldn't believe it. It was a thing that had to do with starting over again. She hoped that the man would understand, but it wasn't easy to get an idea, because the man stood listening, without making a sign, one hand gripping the handle of a small suitcase. His feet were in the wet shoes. Every so often he moved them, because of the irritation. At a certain point he asked the woman how she had had a son at seventeen. That is, if she had chosen to have him, or it had simply happened. The woman shrugged. It's not a nice story, she said, and long ago I decided not to remember it anymore. It can't have been very easy, to forget it, the man observed. Again the woman shrugged her shoulders. I turned the page, she said. The man looked at her for a while, then asked her if she had started over, in the way she dreamed of, with the child in her arms. Yes, the woman answered, and you know what I understood? The man didn't answer. I understood that you never truly change, there's no way to change, the way you are as a child you are your whole life, it's not to change that you start over again. Then what for, asked the man. The woman was silent for a moment. She hadn't realized that the sheet had slid down, below her breasts, or she didn't care. Maybe it was what she wanted. She started over again in order to change tables, she said. One always has this idea of having happened into the wrong game, and that with the cards we have who knows what we could have done if only we had been sitting at a different card table. She had left the child with her mother and had started over with another city, another profession, another way of dressing. Probably she also wanted to leave behind a few things that it wasn't possible to put in place. Now she could no longer remember exactly. But certainly she was tired of losing. As I told you, she added, it's impossible to change your cards, all you can do is change your card table.

Did you find yours? the man asked.

Yes, the woman answered confidently. It's a disgusting table, everyone cheats, the money is dirty, and the people are worthless.

How marvelous.

I couldn't be too fussy, with the cards I hold.

Like?

I'm imprecise, not very intelligent, and too mean. And I've never finished a thing in my life. Is that enough for you?

What do you mean by "mean"?

I don't care about seeing people suffer. Sometimes I like it. Sit down, it's annoying, your standing there, please.

Now I truly have to go.

On the bed. Sit on the bed. You can stay there at the end if it bothers you to get close.

It doesn't bother me, it's that I have to go.

Like that, good.

A moment, then I really have to go. Just tell me how you're going to leave here, tomorrow.

What?

Tomorrow morning, if they see you.

What do I know? I'll make up something. That you picked me up last night and this morning you vanished, taking my wallet. Things like that.

Very kind of you.

Don't mention it.

In fact you have no idea how little it matters to me.

Really?

Really.

That is, you're pretending?

Pretending what?

To be someone who cares what they think of him in a hotel. A half-wit of that type.

No, I really am. It's that now I'm late.

Don't be like that, I was joking, I won't get you in trouble, they won't see me leave, if there's one thing I know how to do it's leave a hotel without anyone noticing, believe me. I was joking.

It's not that.

Then what?

Nothing. It's that it's late now.

For what?

Forget it.

Is it so important, this work thing?

I should have gone earlier. It's that I couldn't get out of that chair.

Maybe you didn't want to.

That's also possible. But it would be extremely illogical for someone like me.

You never do things that are illogical?

No.

Never a mistake?

Many, but never illogical.

There's a difference?

Obviously.

Give me an example.

I would have a perfect one, quite recent, but believe me, it's not something to talk about now.

You smiled.

What?

It's the first time you've smiled since we met. You have a lovely smile, you know?

Thank you.

You ought to do it more often, I mean smile, it gives you that melancholy air that appeals to women.

Are you coming on to me?

Now then!

I'm sorry, it was a joke.

A joke. I hope you can do better.

Yes, I can do better, but not tonight, I'm sorry.

What is there about tonight?

It's the wrong night.

You're here, chatting, with a naked woman in the bed, what's wrong about it, apart from the deplorable absence of alcohol, I mean.

If you like there should be a minibar somewhere.

How can you say "there should be," you've been coming to this hotel for sixteen years and you've never looked to see where the minibar is?

No.

You're crazy.

I don't drink much.

What about water, you've never even felt like having some water?

I usually bring it with me.

Jesus, you're crazy. Do me a favor and go look for this damn minibar. Generally it's under the television.

In fact, that seems to be the most logical solution.

The most logical solution would be next to the bed.

Wrong. The noise wouldn't let you sleep.

But the alcohol, yes.

Beer?

Beer? There's nothing else?

Nothing alcoholic.

What a hotel. There isn't any popcorn, I'm mad about popcorn…

No, nothing to eat.

Disgusting. All right, we'll have to make do with beer. You have one, too.

But the man said he preferred not to drink, he had managed not to for the whole night, and he didn't feel like giving in just now. He said he needed to remain lucid. Then he went toward the bed and while he was crossing the room he noticed the light filtering through the curtains. He turned back and with one hand looked for the cords to open them, remembering how absolutely certain it was, although for incomprehensible reasons, that one would pull the wrong cord, the one that opens when you want to close, or vice versa. He said it to the woman, as wittily as he could, and meanwhile he managed to shift the curtains slightly. It was dawn. He looked at the distant sky brightened by an ambiguous light and wasn't sure of anything. The woman asked if he was hatching that beer, and so he brought it to her. Sit down, said the woman, but in a gentle tone, this time. Just a moment, said the man, and went back to the window. There was that light. He thought it was an invitation, but now it was difficult to understand if it was addressed to him, too. He looked at his watch as if there were some possibility of finding an answer there, and he didn't get anything useful, except the vague impression that it was the wrong time for a lot of things. Maybe he ought still to have faith, leave the room, get in the car, and drive onto a highway, pressing the accelerator. Maybe it would be more appropriate to get in the bed and find out if the body of the woman was really as desirable as it seemed. But this he thought as if it were someone else's idea, not his. He heard the snap of a can that was being opened and then the woman's voice asking if he had always been like that. Like what? Like all in order, said the woman. The man smiled. Then he said no. So the woman wanted to know when he had begun to be like that, if he remembered, and it was for that reason that, without moving from the window, he said that he remembered precisely, he was thirteen and it had all happened in one night. He said that everything had shattered then. In front of his house that was burning, that night, everything had shattered, in the face of that senseless fire. I was thirteen, he said. Then I met a man who taught me to put things in order, and from then on I've never stopped thinking that we have no other task but that. There is always a house to rebuild, he added, and it's a long job, which requires a lot of patience. The woman asked him again to sit on the bed, but he didn't answer and, as if following his thoughts, said that every night his father listened to the radio and drank a bottle of wine, to the bottom. He sat at the table, placed his gun in front of him, and next to it the bottle. He drank with a straw, slowly, and you couldn't disturb him as he was doing it, for any reason. He never touched the gun. He liked to have it there, just that. He said that that night, too, everything had been just like that, the night when the fire consumed everything. Then he asked the woman if she had a house.

Four walls and a bed? Of course.

Not in that sense. A true house. In your head.

I'm not sure I understand.

Something you're building, your task.

Ah, that.

Yes, that.

I told you, I never finish anything.

Did you ever start, at least, once?

Maybe once.

Where was it?

Next to a man.

It's a good point of departure.

Well.

The father of the child?

Him? Hardly, he was a real dickhead, at the right opportunity he disappeared.

I'm sorry.

He didn't even have a job. Or maybe he did, but something like stealing cars.

And the other?

Who?

The man of the house.

Well, him…

Was there something special about him?

Everything. There's only him, in the world.

Meaning?

There's no one like him.

Where is he now?

Not with me.

Why?

Forget it.

He didn't love you?

Oh yes, he loved me.

So?

We made a real mess of things.

Like?

You wouldn't understand.

Why?

Do you have an idea what it means to be mad about someone?

I'm afraid not.

There.

Try to explain it to me.

Are you joking?

Try, just tell me even one thing.

Why?

I don't have anything else to do. I have to wait for the shoes to dry.

That's a good answer. What is it you want to know, exactly?

What it means to be mad about someone.

You don't know.

No.

The only thing that occurred to the woman was that you understand all films about love, you *truly* understand them. But that wasn't easy to explain, either. And it sounded a bit foolish. Involuntarily there returned to her mind many scenes she had lived through beside the man she loved, or far from him, which after all was the same thing—it had been for a long time. Usually she tried not to think about it. But now they came to mind, and in particular she remembered one of the last times they parted and what she had understood at that moment—she was sitting at a table in a café, and he had just left. What she had understood, with absolute certainty, was that to live without him would be, forever, her fundamental occupation, and that from that moment on things would always have a shadow for her, an extra shadow, even in the dark, and maybe especially in the dark. She wondered if that might work as an explanation of what it means to be mad about someone, but looking up at the man standing at the window, there with his suitcase in hand, she saw it as so elementary and final that it seemed to her totally pointless to try to explain. All in all she didn't have a great desire to, and she wasn't there for that. So she smiled a sad smile that wasn't hers and said no, it was better to forget about it. Be kind, she said to the man, let's not talk about me anymore. As you like, said the man. The woman opened another can of beer and was silent for a while. Then she asked how in the world a person ends up building scales. It didn't really interest her, but she wanted to put a stop to the silence, or maybe to the memory of the man she loved. So she asked how someone ends up building scales. It must have seemed an important question to the man, because he began to recall when he had first been taught to measure. To measure correctly. He had liked what you did with your hands, to measure correctly. Probably it was then that he had become obsessed with the idea that there was a lack of tools for measuring, and that that was the beginning of any problem. He had to measure two paints and mix them, measure exactly how much it took of one and how much of the other. If you did it right the brush would glide over the wood, and the color would be just right in the morning light and slightly warmer in the light of sunset. He would have liked to explain that this had to do with the task we all have of rebuilding our house, and was in a certain sense the beginning of it, its dawn. But as he searched for the words he looked down at the street and saw that three police cars had stopped at the entrance to the hotel, their blue lights flashing. One policeman had gotten out and was leaning against the open door, and talking on a radio. The man stopped speaking and turned to the woman, there in the bed. Only in that moment did he notice her eyes, which were pale but gray, like a wolf's, and he understood where her beauty began. I'm listening, said the woman. The man kept staring at her—those eyes—but finally he went back to looking out the window and began to remember again the two cans of paint, and the thick liquid that came out into a glass measuring cup.

It took some time to learn, he said finally.

You're strange, said the woman. Come here.

No.

Why?

The night is over.

You're not still thinking of that damn appointment? They must have given you up for dead by now.

It's not that.

So? Are you afraid they'll catch you, tomorrow morning, with a woman in an evening dress? I told you I can vanish and they won't even notice.

Really?

Of course.

Maybe you should do it now.

I wouldn't think of it! Why?

Believe me, do it now.

What are you talking about?

Nothing.

In fact, you know what I'm going to do? What we need is a nice breakfast here in the room, to celebrate.

Put down that phone.

What's the number of the reception desk?

Don't do that, please.

Nine, here, it's always…

Put down that phone.

Calm down, what's got into you?

Put it down immediately!

All right… all right, here, done.

I'm sorry.

What's wrong with you?

It wasn't a good idea.

Certainly it was.

Believe me, it wasn't.

I wasn't going to ask for two, I'd ask for one, we'd share it, and when they brought it up I'd go hide in the bathroom.

For a moment the man seemed to think that it might actually work, but that wasn't in fact what he was thinking. He was about to say something when they knocked on the door, three times. From the corridor a voice said County Police, unemphatic but loud, without hesitation. The man was silent for a moment, then he said aloud, I'm coming. He turned to look at the woman. She was motionless; the sheets had slid down to her hips. The man took off his jacket, went to the bed, and handed it to the woman. Cover up, he said. They knocked again at the door. The woman put on the jacket, looked at the man, and said softly, You mustn't worry. The man shook his head no. Then he said aloud, I'm coming, and went toward the door. The woman put her hands in the pockets of the jacket and with her right hand felt a gun. She grasped it. The man opened the door.

County Police, said the policeman, showing a badge. He kept the other hand on the butt of a gun that was hanging from his belt.

Are you Mr. Malcolm Webster? asked the policeman.

Yes, I am, said the man.

I must ask you to follow me, said the policeman.

Then he turned toward the bed and didn't seem surprised to find the woman, under the covers.

The gun? he asked her.

Everything's okay, the woman answered. I have it.

The policeman nodded assent.

He turned again to the man.

Let's go, he said.

2.

She was a girl, and dressing like a woman made her seem even younger. The makeup, too: the lipstick and the heavy lines around the eyes—pale eyes, but gray, like a she-wolf. She arrived around nine in the evening, with her boyfriend, someone who was evidently her boyfriend, quite a bit older. They must have had a lot to drink already. They hadn't reserved, and to the hotel clerk they said they had left their documents in the car. The clerk was a man around sixty who had been instructed by the management not to be too fussy and to demand payment in advance. He wasn't a man who could afford to act on his own, so he gave the two a room on the third floor and asked for the payment. The boy took a wad of bills out of his pocket and paid in cash. While he was doing it, he added some rather crude remarks, because he liked it to be understood that he was a toughie. The girl said nothing. She was standing a little distance away.

They went up to the room but almost immediately came down again and went out to dinner without saying anything.

It was a fairly dingy hotel, on the outskirts of the city.

In the middle of the night the hotel clerk, lying on his cot, heard some noises in the lobby, like muffled voices. He got up to investigate and he saw the two of them leaning against a wall, kissing. The girl looked as if she wanted to go up to the room, but he kept her crushed against the wall and she giggled between one kiss and the next. The boy stuck a hand under her skirt and then she closed her eyes, still laughing. It could have been an amusing scene, but the boy had a manner that wasn't very nice. The hotel clerk gave a slight cough. The boy turned toward him and then went back to doing what he was doing, as if it didn't matter to him that someone was looking at him, or as if he liked it. But the clerk didn't like it, and so he took the key to their room and said aloud that he would be grateful if they would go up. The boy cursed, but took his hand away and used it to straighten his hair. Finally they took the key and left. The clerk remained standing behind the desk, and was thinking that there was something delightful about the girl when she reappeared in the lobby, with a shadow of weariness she hadn't had before, and said there were no towels in the room. The clerk was sure there were but went to get some in the storeroom without wondering what the story was. He returned with the towels and gave them to the girl, who thanked him politely, and moved as if to go. But after a couple of steps she stopped and, turning to the man, asked a question, as if she had been saving it up for a long time, and in a tone in which there was simple curiosity and a little of that weariness.

When do night clerks sleep? she asked.

At night, the man answered.

Oh.

In bits and pieces, of course.

All you night clerks are in bits and pieces, then.

Yes, in the sense that we have to wake up and go back to sleep many times.

How did you end up in a job like this?

I wasn't in a position to choose. And then I don't dislike it.

Certainly being a rock star would be something else.

Certainly I wouldn't have the tranquility and the time that I have the privilege of having at my disposal here.

What?

I mean that I like it here. I wanted to be tranquil.

Suit yourself. In my opinion you didn't have the balls to dream of something better. Good night.

Odd, it's the same thing I thought about you.

Excuse me?

When I saw you come in, and then afterward, there, in the lobby, I thought it was a pity.

What was a pity?

That boy. You with that boy. You, if I may say, are a charming girl, it's immediately obvious.

What nonsense are you talking?

I'm sorry. I wish you good night.

No, now tell me what you meant.

It's not important.

I'm sure, but now tell me anyway.

Your boyfriend will be expecting the towels.

My business. What's this story of the charming girl?

You keep your feet right next to one another—attached. Girls don't always know that if they're wearing high heels the way to stand, when they're not moving, is with their feet together. Sometimes it's the width of a finger, but that's not the same thing.

Listen to this.

They don't all understand, but you know it, and then all the rest, too, you have a nice way of… of everything. Your boyfriend, on the other hand, is all wrong, no?

And you—you understand?

And so I thought it was a pity. I thought maybe you didn't have the balls to dream of something better.

You should sleep a little more, you know? You're really not well.

It may be. But certain things can be understood.

And what do you think you understand?

Certain things.

What is it, did you go to school, are you a psychologist during the day, or a fortune-teller?

No. It's that I'm of a certain age, and I've seen all kinds of things.

Standing behind the front desk of a hotel?

Partly.

What kind of experience is that?

I've had others.

Such as?

Having children like you.

Big deal.

Does that seem worthless to you?

Anyone's capable of having children.

That's true. I was in jail. Do you like that?

You, in jail?

Thirteen years.

Are you making fun of me?

I wouldn't dare.

You don't seem like the jail type.

No, it's true.

Did you end up there by mistake?

I ended up there for a whole series of reasons that lined up in an anomalous and uncorrectable way.

I don't understand.

I killed a man.

Shit.

Your boyfriend is waiting for you.

You killed a man how?

I shot him. One shot, just one.

What aim…

It was at a few feet, it wasn't exactly easy to miss. But the fact that I'd fired just one shot helped, in court.

You give the impression that you didn't really enjoy it.

Right.

Something tidy.

So to speak.

Why did you kill him?

It's a long story.

All right, make it short.

Why should I tell you?

I don't know, I'd like to know.

Let's do like this…

Yes, but hurry, I have to go.

I'll tell you the story, but in exchange you'll leave this hotel, right now, without even saying goodbye to the man up there.

What?

I said that I would be glad to tell you why I killed him, but afterward, in exchange, I'd like you to leave and go home.

What the fuck are you talking about?

I don't honestly know. But this idea occurred to me. I'd very much like to see you go out that door and find a better place.

What's wrong with this place?

That man.

My boyfriend?

Maybe. You and him, yes. That's all wrong.

Listen to you.

Maybe I'm wrong.

Of course you're wrong.

You're sure?

Of course.

Then I'm sorry. Take the towels. Good night.

Just a minute, just a minute.

Go.

Just a minute. The story first.

I said that I would be glad to tell you, but in exchange you must do me the kindness of leaving through that door and going home.

What's with you, idiot? Surely you don't think that I'll really do it? Leave just because you'd *like* it.

In fact I see it as an unlikely possibility.

You could even say impossible.

Why?

It's my life, what do you have to do with it?

Apart from that?

Apart from that, in any case I couldn't go.

Why?

He'd beat me up.

Ah, there.

Satisfied?

No. Not at all. How did you get into this situation?

How do I know.

Fantastic.

I liked… that is, I *like*, except that…

What do you like?

My boyfriend.

Yes, but what do you like about him?

What a stupid question, I like him, how he looks, I like that he's crazy, I like him in bed. You know what I'm talking about?

I think I can get an idea.

Okay, then get it.

Wasn't there someone less inclined to vulgarity and violence?

What the fuck are you saying?

Why don't you find a nice man who doesn't beat you?

Are there any?

You are splendid.

Forget about it. Give me those towels.

Here.

I think I need a good shower.

Probably.

I'll have to do it without finding out how the hell an idiot like you ended up as a murderer.

Go home and take the shower, and you'll find out.

At home? You have no idea.

You must have a house.

It's not my house, it's my mother's.

In general it doesn't matter.

Answer, it's certainly him.

Reception, good evening… Yes, she's here…I have no idea… Yes, I'll give her to you.

Hello… I'm coming… I stopped to chat a moment… With the clerk… Yes, chat… He could be my grandfather, Mike… That's my business, isn't it… No, look… I told you I'm coming… *Leave me in peace for a minute*? I told you I'm coming… *You're the one who's shouting!*… What do you mean half an hour, it must be five minutes… What do I know, it must be at the bottom of my purse… Don't shout, please… *Don't shout, shit…* I said… fuck off.

I'm sorry, it's my fault.

What the fuck…

Go on.

No, call him back for me, please.

On the telephone?

If not, then what? Hurry up.

I really think that…

Hurry up, or else he'll come down!

Here.

Hello?… Hello?… Sorry, sorry, please, I'm sorry… Mike… right… I'm coming right up… I swear… I've just got the towels…

I love you… yes… I told you… yes, I'm coming.

Now go.

Yes, I'm going.

Good night.

You weren't kidding me, right?

In what sense?

You really were in jail.

Thirteen years.

Thirteen?

I read a lot. They passed.

I'd go mad inside.

You're young, it's different. Go.

How old do you think I am?

Eighteen. You wrote it, on the form you filled out for the hotel.

And you believe it?

No.

So?

You tell me.

Sixteen.

Goodness.

Everyone says it's a special age.

Yes, it seems to be.

You think it's a special age?

I don't know, I never was that age.

You skipped it?

So to speak.

Too bad.

It's also too bad to throw your life away the way you're doing.

I'm not throwing it away in the least.

I'm sorry, you're right, I don't know anything about it.

Why do you say I'm throwing it away?

I don't know. Your face.

What about my face?

It's very beautiful.

And so?

It would be very beautiful if it didn't have that mean look.

Mean?

You have a mean face.

Cool!

Well.

I *am* mean.

As long as you're satisfied.

Yes, I am satisfied, I like being mean, it protects me from the world, it's the reason I'm not afraid of anything. What's wrong with being mean?

The man thought a moment. Then he said that you have to pay attention when you're young because the light you live in when you're young is the light you'll live in forever, for a reason he had never understood. But he knew it was so. He said that many people, for example, are depressed in their youth, and then they remain so forever. Or they grow up in a half-light and the half-light follows them all their life. So you have to pay attention to meanness, because when you're young it seems a luxury you can afford, but the truth is different, and that is that meanness is a cold light in which everything loses color, and loses it forever. He also said that he, for example, had grown up in violence and tragedy, and he had to admit that through a series of circumstances he had never managed to escape from that light, although in general he could say that he had done things properly, in the course of his life, with the sole intention of putting them in order, and basically succeeding, but undeniably in a light that had never been other than tragic and violent, with rare moments of beauty, which he would never forget. Then he saw the elevator descending from the third floor to the ground floor and he realized that something on the girl's face had hardened, something very similar to a small spasm of fear. Instinctively the man wanted to go back into his little room, but then he thought he couldn't leave the girl there, and so he said to her, Quick, come with me, and she, oddly, followed and let him lead her into the office, where the man signaled to her to be quiet while he looked around for something— he wouldn't have been able to say what it was. He heard the door of the elevator open and the voice of the boy shouting the girl's name. The man waited a moment, then came out of the room and went to the desk. The boy was in underpants and a T-shirt. The man looked at him with all the impersonal mildness he was capable of.

I must ask you not to shout, he said.

I'll shout as much as I want. Where is she?

Who?

My girlfriend.

I don't know. She took the towels.

And where did she go?

I don't know, I think she went upstairs.

When?

After you called her, on the phone, she took the towels, then I don't know.

And what are these?

These?

Are you an idiot? These, *these*, aren't they towels?

She must have left them here. I don't know, I was busy, I went back to my—

What the fuck?

She must have forgotten them.

Where did she go?

Maybe she went up to the terrace for a moment.

What terrace?

I told her there was a terrace on the top floor, where it's very beautiful at night, you can see the whole city lit up. Maybe she felt like—

The terrace?

I don't know, if she didn't go back to the room...

How do you get to this goddamn terrace?

You take the elevator to the top floor and then there's one more flight of stairs. The door is open.

Now, tell me. You're sure you didn't see her go out?

Out of the hotel?

Out of the hotel, yes, am I speaking Arabic?

She may have, but as I was saying I was busy and so I went back in there and...

Don't try to make me an idiot, you know?

I'm only doing my job.

Shit job.

I have thought so at times, yes.

Okay, good, think so every so often, it won't hurt you.

Your towels.

Fuck you.

You won't take them?

You old fool…

Then the boy said nothing else. He headed toward the elevator, but something occurred to him that made him take the stairs, cursing in a low voice. The man didn't move. He realized only at that moment that his hands were trembling and he was glad that the boy hadn't noticed. He stood there for a moment, because he wasn't sure that the boy wouldn't come back, and he tried to think quickly what he should do now. Nothing occurred to him. What an idiot, he thought, but he didn't mean the boy. He went back to the room and this time he knew the girl's name. Mary Jo, he said, now it would be best if you go up, quickly. She was sitting on the cot. She kept her feet together, in that nice way she had. She shook her head no. I'm afraid, she said. Of what, asked the man. Of going upstairs.

Then leave, but hurry, said the man.

I'm afraid of that, too.

I'll go with you.

It makes no sense.

Why?

I have to go back upstairs.

But instead you'll leave, it's the right thing to do, I'll go with you.

You have to stay here.

No one will notice.

And then where the fuck do I go?

We don't have time to discuss it now. Come on.

Forget it. It's over.

Come on, I told you.

Why?

Look outside, it's already dawn.

So?

It's time you went home to bed.

What does the time have to do with it, I'm not a child.

It's not a question of time, it's a question of light.

What the hell do you mean?

It's the right light for going home, it's made just for that.

The light?

There's no better light in which to feel yourself cleansed. Let's go.

You don't really think that.

Yes, I do. Come with me.

We don't even know where the fuck to go!

We'll improvise. To the station, maybe. They open early. We both need a good coffee, don't you think? Come, we'll go out the back. Do you mind leaving the towels?

I wouldn't think of it. I'll take them with me.

As you like, but hurry up, this way.

I love stealing hotel towels.

Very childish.

No way. What do you think, I take them to be rude?

I don't see any other reason. As towels they're nothing special. Come on, let's turn this way.

The quality isn't important. It's that later, at home, they remind me of where I've been. Can you understand that?

A souvenir?

Sort of.

Cumbersome, as a souvenir.

True. Will you hold them for me? Thank you.

But walk a little more quickly, please.

Are we in a hurry?

I don't know.

What light, anyway.

I told you.

And in fact, on that summer morning, dawn spread over the clear sky with such assurance that even those unambitious suburbs seemed taken by surprise, yielding to a sort of beauty that they had not been built for. There were optimistic gleams on the windows, and the thin grass shone, where it was, with an unexpected green. Even the few passing cars seemed to have suspended any particular haste, as if they had been given a respite. The man and the girl walked beside each other, and it was an odd sight, because the girl was pretty and the man very ordinary, besides old. You would have struggled to figure out the story, seeing them, she in her high heels, her steps confident, he slightly bent, with a set of white towels under his arm. Maybe a father and daughter, but not even. Leaving the main street, they skirted the walls of an old brewery, and the man didn't say that he had chosen that way because there was still the fear of the boy in underpants, and the certainty that he wouldn't find the terrace, since there wasn't one. He preferred to talk about the brewery, and the odor of malt and of pubs you could still smell, passing by. He recounted that the owner had run off to the Caribbean, three years earlier, and for a while the workers had managed the brewery themselves, and hadn't done too badly, but then things went as they were bound to go. The girl asked if he'd ever drunk that beer, and the man said he hadn't had a drink for years, he couldn't allow himself to, because he was on probation and if anything stupid happened he'd end up back in jail in the blink of an eye. So I prefer to remain lucid, he said. In any case, I'd like it to be something stupid that I chose to do lucidly, he added. Maybe he was referring, remotely, to what he was doing at that moment. The girl must have thought so, too, because immediately she said that he could go back to the hotel now, she would manage. But the man shook his head no, without adding anything. He was so evidently helpless, in his tranquility, that the girl loved him, for a moment. Only then did she realize that he was in fact risking losing his job, walking at dawn around an abandoned brewery, beside a crazy girl, and strangely the situation didn't please her. Suddenly it was important to her that that man not suffer, and following her thoughts she went so far as to think that she would like him never to have suffered in life. So at a certain point she asked the man if they had waited for him, his family, during those years in prison.

More or less, the man answered.

Yes or no?

My wife more or less. And the children, one was already grown up, he left, the other two stayed with their mother.

You mean when you came out you no longer had a home of your own.

We tried it for a while, but it didn't work. Many things had changed.

Such as?

I had changed. They had, too. All. It isn't easy.

Were they ashamed of you?

No, I don't think so, *ashamed* isn't the right word. Maybe a term that has to do with forgiveness would be more appropriate.

They didn't forgive you.

Something like that. It's too bad, because in fact I had done it for them.

What?

It's for them that I killed that man.

Seriously?

Yes. For myself, for them. To protect my house.

I can't manage if you walk so fast.

I'm sorry.

We're not in a hurry, are we?

I don't know.

My boyfriend?

Him.

Bah. Continue the story.

What?

You owe me a story.

Right.

So?

He was a loan shark. The man I killed was a loan shark.

Wow!

You know what I'm talking about?

Of course, I'm not an idiot. A loan shark.

I owed him a lot of money. He would have gotten angry with my children.

And so you shot him.

Yes.

How stupid, they threaten, but when the moment comes they don't do anything. It's their system.

Not in this case.

How do you know?

He began with irritating things, nothing violent, but unpleasant. Warnings.

And you got frightened.

No. I was calm. But I couldn't come up with the money, and he kept it up. He knew everything about us, schedules, places, everything.

You could report him.

Sooner or later it would come out and then he would find us. That's how it works. If you report it, you'll pay for that later.

What shit. You know where we're going, right?

More or less.

Okay. Then go on.

Nothing, I asked for it, I needed the money, and found myself in that mess.

And nothing occurred to you except to shoot him?

There was no other way out, believe me. Killing him was the only move that could end the game.

And you came up with a plan?

More or less. I tried to figure out if there was something in which I was stronger than him.

And you found it.

Yes. I had more imagination and the face of a coward.

You mean?

He would never have expected that I could do something

courageous, or violent. So I told him that I had the money, decide a place; he didn't even take the trouble to choose carefully, or to have someone accompany him. He arrived, I approached, and I shot him. It was the last thing he would have expected.

Shit.

That's how it happened.

Didn't it… I mean, didn't it upset you? To shoot, I mean.

I grew up in a world in which people shot. My father was an accountant, but when it was necessary he'd shoot.

Seriously?

It was a world like that. People killed each other, and did it normally.

In what sense *normally*?

That's another story that I don't owe you.

All right. Then finish mine.

What do you still want to know?

What you did, afterward. Did you run away, did you go to the police, what did you do?

I got in the car and for a couple of days I wandered around. The first day I had some appointments with clients, I kept them. Then enough, I wandered around and that's all. I didn't even call home.

You ran away.

No, I wandered around. But I didn't hide even for a moment. I didn't care if they caught me.

Why?

I still had the gun with me. I kept it in my jacket pocket. I thought sooner or later of killing myself.

Really?

That was the idea. It was a logical idea.

But then you didn't do it.

I thought I'd do it when I saw the police arriving. But they were very clever.

How?

They imagined something like that, and so they were very clever. They followed me for a while from a distance, then they chose their moment well. I was in a hotel and they came to get me there, at dawn, but in a nice way, politely. I was lucky, they were policemen who knew their job.

So you didn't shoot yourself.

As you see.

Maybe it would have been better if you'd shot yourself.

Who knows. But I would rather rule it out. It's always better to be alive.

Even in prison?

But the man didn't answer, because a black car, a few intersections farther on, stopped suddenly and went into reverse. Is it him? asked the man, and the girl nodded yes. She had turned pale. Over here, said the man, and they began to run toward the avenue, where more cars were passing and maybe there were also people. The girl bent down to take off her shoes and, holding them in her hand, began to run fast. The man's heart was pounding in his ears, he was trying to think, to come up with an idea. He was sure that the boy had seen them, but probably he was so angry that it would take him a while to orient himself in that web of narrow streets. Maybe they still had a few minutes, although it wasn't clear what they could do with them. Maybe reaching the avenue was already something, he thought, and when they got there he turned to see if the black car had arrived first. A bus was approaching, with the arrow flashing. He turned and saw the bus stop twenty yards away. Here, quick, he shouted to the girl, and meanwhile he raised his arm so that the bus would see them. They reached the stop, and the time the bus took to brake and open its doors seemed an eternity. Get in, hurry, said the man. The girl got in without saying a word. The man instinctively reached a hand into his pocket for a ticket, because he was that type of man. But there wasn't time, because the doors closed. From behind the glass the girl shouted something and he thought she was asking why in the world he hadn't gotten on. He shook his head no. The bus left, and he saw the girl waving at him. It seemed to him that she did it gracefully, as she probably did everything.

Then he stood there, his heart pounding. He wasn't even thinking.

A minute, maybe, or a little more, and the black car stopped in front of him. The door opened and the boy got out, calm, slowly. He wasn't in underpants and a T-shirt, he was dressed. He walked around the car and approached the man. She's pregnant, asshole, he whispered softly, then he punched the man in the ribs, and the man crumpled to the ground. He huddled on the sidewalk, like an insect, and meanwhile he thought of jail and what he could do to avoid ending up there again. Don't do anything, he thought. The boy kicked him in the back, repeating in a low voice, Asshole. Then he took a cigarette and lighted it. The man, on the ground, was listening to his own heart. He felt the boy take a few steps, as if to move away. Then he heard him close by again.

Where did she go? the boy asked.

To the man it seemed that the news that the girl was pregnant changed things a little.

She took the bus, he answered.

The boy gave an ambiguous nod of the head. He took a furious drag on his cigarette.

Get up, he said.

The man thought he would never make it, but the boy repeated get up and he did it in a cruel, impatient voice. So the man planted his arms on the sidewalk and with immense effort stood up. He felt a pain in his chest that cracked him in two.

Get in the car, said the boy, in that same voice.

The man raised his head and for a moment wondered where were those few passersby he remembered walking hurriedly along the avenue. He got in the car and it occurred to him that he might not get out alive. But it was a stupid idea, probably.

The boy sat behind the wheel and the man, next to him, slumped against the seat back. Nothing happened for a while. Then the boy started the engine and slowly made a U-turn, setting off along the avenue. They drove as if they had no goal, and maybe they didn't. But finally the boy turned onto a street he recognized and after about fifty yards stopped in front of the hotel. He turned off the engine, pulled down the window, and lighted a cigarette. He was silent for a while.

I'm not even sure it's mine, he said at a certain point. The child, he added.

Why?

What do you mean, why? You saw what type of girl she is.

She's sweet.

She's crazy.

But in a lovely way, said the man, and then he began to cough, because of the thing that was cracked in his chest.

The boy let him cough, then asked if he had children.

More or less, the man answered.

I don't want a child who isn't mine, said the boy.

Then they said nothing until the boy said, Get out, and he said it as if he didn't care about anything anymore.

The man opened the door and said, I'm sorry.

Scram, said the boy. He didn't even wait until the man had really gotten out, he reached over to close the door and took off, tires screeching.

The man stood there, in front of the hotel. He looked around and was surprised to see a light that was still imbued with the dawn, because it seemed to him that hours had passed since he left with the girl. He didn't move, because the pain was piercing, but also because he had the vague sensation of having forgotten something. The towels came to mind. He imagined them on the ground, at the bus stop. He pictured them white and smooth, there on the ground, and for a moment he thought it was good that the boy had beaten him without causing him to bleed. He wouldn't have liked the white towels to be stained with blood. And now, instead, he could imagine them clean, and mysterious, in the curious gaze of the passersby.

Someone will pick them up and take them home, he thought.

3.

The boy had lain down on the bed without even taking off his shoes, and had been tossing on top of the covers, falling asleep from time to time, but it wasn't a real sleep. Sitting on a chair, in a corner of the room, a woman observed him, trying to get rid of the annoying sensation that they weren't doing the right thing. She hadn't taken off her coat, because even the heating was terrible in that depressing hotel. Like the dirty carpet and the framed jigsaw puzzles on the walls. Only those idiot bosses of hers could have thought it was a good idea to take a thirteen-year-old boy there, after what he had endured that night. The stupidity of the police. All because they hadn't been able to track down a relative to take him to. They had found only an uncle, who, however, had no intention of budging from where he was, that is, a construction site in the North, an asshole. So now here she was playing nanny to the boy, in that shitty hotel, and in the morning something would be decided. But the boy tossed and turned, on top of the covers, and the woman couldn't stand that abandonment, and the sadness of everything. No boy could deserve shit like that. She got up and went over to the bed. It's cold, she said, get under the covers. The boy shook his head no. He didn't even open his eyes. First they had talked a little, and she even managed to make him laugh. Suppose that I'm your grandmother, she had said. You're not that old, he had said. I look good for my age, the woman had said; she was fifty-six and in fact felt every one of her years. Then she had tried to get him to sleep, and now there she was, convinced that it was all wrong.

She went to the bathroom to wash her face, because it was important to stay awake. And she had an idiotic idea that, however, made her immediately feel better. She turned it over in her mind, and knew that it was full of holes, but she also liked it because it was crazy and delicate. She went back to the chair, still thinking, and since the boy continued to toss and turn on the bed, at a certain point she said Fuck, rose, picked up her bag, and turned on the lights. The boy opened his eyes and looked at her. Let's go, said the woman. Get your stuff, we're going. The boy put his feet down and looked around. Where? he asked. To a better place, said the woman.

They left the hotel and got into an old Honda, parked in back. It didn't have police markings and didn't seem in great shape. It was a beat-up squad car that at the precinct only she used. She was attached to it. She loaded the stuff in the trunk, told the boy to get in, and took the wheel. You stretch out and try to sleep, she said to the boy. Then she slowly left the parking lot, checking that there was no police car in the vicinity. She relaxed a little only when they turned onto the road that led out of the city. The boy hadn't asked questions, and seemed more interested in the radio installed on the dashboard than in the purpose of that journey into the night. Once they were in the countryside there was really nothing to see out the windows, where everything was devoured by the darkness. While the woman drove silently the boy curled up on the seat and closed his eyes. Sleep, said the woman.

She drove for a good hour, trying to concentrate on the road, because she had never liked driving and was afraid of falling asleep. There was no traffic; at that hour of the night it was something if you came across a sleepless truck. But for the woman it was difficult anyway, because she wasn't used to that kind of thing, and all that darkness made her nervous. So she was glad when she saw the boy sit up and look around, while he stretched like an ordinary boy, one who hadn't been through what he had. It seemed to the woman that everything was going a little better.

Hello, kiddo, she said.

Where are we?

Almost there. Do you want some water?

No.

There should be some cans under the seat.

No, I'm okay.

You remember, right, who I am?

Yes.

Detective Pearson.

Yes.

You just have to relax and I'll take care of the rest. You trust me?

Where's my jacket?

Everything's in the trunk. I took everything.

Why didn't we stay there?

It was a terrible hotel. It wasn't a good idea to stay there.

I want to go home.

Malcolm—your name is Malcolm, right?

Yes.

Going home is also not a good idea, Malcolm, believe me.

I want to see my house.

You'll see it. But not tonight.

Why?

There's no need to talk about it now.

Why?

We can talk about something else.

Like?

Soccer, cars. Or you can ask me questions.

Who are you?

A detective, you know that.

A *lady* detective?

It's not forbidden, you know.

Yes, but… how did you think of it?

Oh, that. At a certain point I changed everything and the idea occurred to me. I wanted to start over again. I was with a policeman. There was an exam and I passed.

Was it hard?

Nonsense.

Even shooting?

Even that.

Did you ever shoot, afterward?

At first. But I wasn't the type to enjoy it. I liked other things more.

Like?

Understanding. I liked to understand. And then I liked the criminals. The crazies. I liked to understand them. At one point I began to study. It's the only thing I *almost* finished in my life. They used me for that, at the police.

For that what?

When they needed to understand the minds of criminals or crazy people. I stopped shooting and for quite a while they used me for other things, where there was no need for guns. I was the type of policeman they send to the roof to talk to people who are going to jump, you know?

Yes.

They called me when there were letters from maniacs to read.

Cool.

I was good at it, then.

Why do you keep saying I *was* good at it?

I say what?

I *did* this, I *did* that… aren't you a cop anymore?

I am, but I stopped doing anything good long ago.

Who said so?

Me, I said it.

Excuse me a moment… 3471, Detective Pearson… Yes, the boy is with me… I know… I know perfectly well… It wasn't a good idea… I know what the orders were, but it wasn't a good idea, does it seem to you a good idea to keep a boy all night in that wretched hotel after what happened to him? Is that what you'd call a good idea?… I know… Well, you know what you can do with your rules?… Do what you want, you know how much of a damn I give about it… He's here with me, I told you… No, I'm not telling you, but it's the right place for him… Make all the reports you want, then I'll make one, too… What kidnapping, what the hell are you talking about, I'm only taking him… No, I'm not going back, let's end it here… Do what you want… You know how much of a damn I give… Fuck off, Stoner, over and out.

Sorry, kiddo.

That's okay.

Sorry for the curse words.

That's okay.

They can't do anything to me.

No?

Four days and I'm done. I turn in the badge and retire. They can't do anything to me. You might be my last job—I want to do it well and in my own way.

Do the police retire?

If they don't get knocked off first.

Knocked off?

Killed.

Oh.

Let's do like this, push that button, the first on the left, and turn off the radio. That way they won't interrupt us anymore.

This one?

Yes. Good.

Is there also a siren?

Yes, but it's broken. There's the blue light, if you want.

The blue light that spins on the roof?

Yes. It should be under the seat. With the cans.

I'd like it.

Okay. Take it out.

This?

Open the window and stick it on the roof.

It won't fly off?

I hope not. It's supposed to be magnetic. But I haven't used it for a while.

Done.

Put up the window, that's a bitter cold coming in. Okay, let's turn it on. Voilà. Cool, no?

It's really the police light.

You like it?

I don't know.

Something's wrong?

There were all lights like that, in front of the house.

If you don't like it let's take it down.

I don't know.

You don't like it, kiddo, let's take it down.

There was the big light of the fire and then all those lights came.

Take it down, go ahead.

Sorry.

For what? They're horrible lights, you're right.

Where should I put it?

Throw it back there, but put up that window.

There were all those faces I'd never seen, and that blue light on them all. Then there was the smell.

Let's talk about something else.

No.

When we get there we'll talk about it if you want.

No, now.

I'm not sure it's a good idea.

Did someone set it on fire?

We don't know.

A house doesn't catch fire by itself.

It can happen. An electrical wire, a stove left on.

Someone set it on fire. Was it friends of my father?

I don't know. But we'll find out.

You'll find out?

I'm retiring, Malcolm. That shit Stoner will take care of it. He's a shit but he's good at what he does.

You have to tell him that it didn't catch fire by itself, our house.

Okay.

They burned it down.

Okay.

Suddenly there was fire everywhere. I saw it.

Okay.

My parents were fighting. When they fight I go out.

Yes, it's a good system, I also used it.

I jumped off the sidewalk, on my bike, in front of the house. Then came that fire. I left the bike there and went closer. I looked through the big window...

...

...

...

What's strange is that they didn't escape.

Who?

My father and mother. They did nothing to escape. My father

was sitting at the table, with his bottle of wine, and the gun lying next to it, as usual. My mother had come out of the kitchen and was standing in front of him. And they were shouting. But they didn't...

Okay, now let's talk about something else, Malcolm.

No.

Malcolm...

They were shouting at each other. They were shouting on top of each other. And meanwhile everything was on fire.

Okay.

They wouldn't have died if instead of shouting at each other they had run away. Why didn't they?

I don't know, Malcolm.

That's why I couldn't move. I looked at them. I couldn't move. Everything started getting hot, so I began walking backward. I stopped where it wasn't hot anymore. But I couldn't help looking.

Get me a can, Malcolm.

Just a minute. Will they ask me why I didn't go in and save them?

No, they won't ask you.

Tell them it's because I saw that thing.

Okay.

I didn't see my father, but my mother was like a torch, she caught fire at a certain point, but even then she didn't start running away, she stood there like a torch.

Then the woman took one hand off the wheel and placed it on one of the boy's hands. She gripped it hard. She slowed down a little because she seldom drove and wasn't confident, she didn't like driving with a single hand. In the dark, on that road in the emptiness. But

she kept her hand tight on the boy's, being careful not to swerve—
she wanted to tell him to stop it, but also that if he wanted to keep
going she would hold him by the hand. He said again that at the end
there was nothing left of the house, and asked her how it was possible that nothing could remain of a house, after fire had seized it,
in the darkness of the night. The woman knew the exact answer was
that a lot of things about that house would remain forever, and that
he would spend a lifetime getting it out of his head, but instead she
said yes, it was possible, if a house was of wood it could be reduced
to a pile of ashes, however strange that might seem, if one night a fire
decided to consume it, if the hearth in the living room caught fire at
night. It was all smoking, he said. It will smoke for a very long time,
she thought. And she wondered if there is a possibility, a single one,
of returning to look from a distance when we always, all of us, have
some smoking ruin before us, and that boy more than any other.
I am a terrible driver with just one hand, she said. The boy took her
hand and placed it on the wheel. I can manage, he said. Then they
were silent for a long time. There was that road leading eastward,
without ever turning, or just slightly, to avoid a patch of woods. In
the light of the headlights it revealed itself little by little, like a secret
of small importance. They occasionally met a car, but didn't look
at it. The boy took a can, opened it, offered it to the woman, then
remembered that business of driving with one hand, so he brought
it to her lips and she then burst out laughing and said that no, she
couldn't—there were a ton of things like that she couldn't do, she
said. You know how to drive at night, said the boy. This time, yes,
said the woman.

But I'm doing it just for you, she added.

Thank you.

I'm glad to do it. It's a long time since I did something willingly.

Really?

So willingly, I mean.

You're strange, you don't seem like a cop.

Why?

You're fat.

The world is full of fat policemen.

You're not dressed like a cop.

No.

And this car is gross.

Hey, kiddo, you're talking about a Honda Civic, property of the Birmingham police department.

Inside. The inside is disgusting.

Ah, that.

Yes, that.

Every morning, at headquarters, they wash the cars, but not mine, I don't want mine washed.

You like it like this.

Yes.

There's popcorn everywhere.

I love popcorn. It's not easy to eat it while you're driving.

I understand.

And then you see me like this now, but I was a real knockout, you know?

I didn't say you're ugly.

Right. I'm very beautiful. And I was even more. In all honesty, my tits are famous in all the police stations of the Midlands.

Wow.

I'm joking.

Oh.

But it's true, I was a beautiful woman, I was a very beautiful girl, and then I was a very attractive woman. Now it's something else.

What?

It doesn't matter to me anymore.

I don't believe it.

I know, you don't believe it if it doesn't happen to you. Like a lot of other things.

Do you have a husband?

No.

Children?

I do have one, but I haven't seen him for years. I wasn't very good at being a mother. It went like that.

You were good at being a cop.

Yes, for a certain period, I was.

Then you got fat.

Let's put it that way.

I understand.

I wouldn't be so sure, but all right.

No, really, I understand.

What do you understand?

You're like my parents. When the fire broke out they didn't escape. Why does it happen to you people?

Well, now, what are you talking about?

I don't know.

Damned if I would have stayed to get burned up in that house, believe me.

…

Sorry, I didn't mean that.

It's okay.

I meant that I always escaped when the house was on fire, I swear, I escaped plenty of times, I've done nothing but escape. It's not that.

Then what is it?

Come now, that's a lot of questions.

It was just to find out.

Then find me some popcorn, there should be some on the backseat.

Here?

Somewhere. A family pack already open.

There's nothing.

Look on the floor, it must have fallen off.

Down here?

And what the hell is that?

But she wasn't talking about the popcorn. She was seeing something in the rearview mirror that she didn't like. Hell, she said again. She narrowed her eyes to see better. There was a car, in the distance, behind them, and from the blue light on the roof it appeared to be a police car. That shit Stoner, thought the woman. Then instinctively she pressed the accelerator and bent slightly over the steering wheel, murmuring something. The boy turned and saw the car with the blue light, distant in the darkness. It didn't have a siren, only that blue light. He glanced at the woman and saw her concentrated on driving, her hands gripping the steering wheel. She read the road with her eyes almost half-closed, glancing from time to time in the rearview mirror. The boy turned again and it seemed to him that the car, back there, was closer. Don't turn, the woman said to him, it brings bad luck. She added that when you're followed you shouldn't pay attention to who's following you, you have to focus on your choices, stay clear-headed, and know that if you give your utmost no one will capture you. She talked to relax and because gradually she had begun to slow down, tired. If, on the other hand, you're the one following, what you have to do is repeat everything he does, without stopping to think, thinking wastes time, you just have to repeat what he's doing and when you're within range detach yourself from his brain and make your choice. Nine times out of ten it works, she said. If you don't have a wreck like this under your ass, obviously. She looked in the rearview mirror and saw the police car rolling impassively toward them, like a billiard ball toward the hole. Who knows how he found me, that shit, she said. I told you he's good at what he does, she said. Hide the cans, she said. What cans? The beer, she said. The boy looked around but there really weren't any cans. Maybe they were sliding under the seats, in the midst of the popcorn and all that incredible stuff like the box for a hair dryer, a crumpled poster, two fishing boots. No beer, he said. Good, said the woman, and then she said it would be better if he stretched out on the seat and pretended to sleep. It occurred to her that that would keep Stoner from shouting. It would be better if they avoided shouting. Speaking calmly, maybe she would convince him. She looked in the rearview mirror and saw that the blue light was now flashing fifty yards away. I can't manage to do anything right anymore, she thought. And she was seized by the anguish that suffocated her at night, in the sleepless hours, when every piece of her life passed through her mind, and there wasn't one in which a creeping, inevitable end wasn't written. She took her foot off the accelerator slightly and the car behind closed in. The boy had shut his eyes, the blue flashes under his eyelids, closer and closer. The police car put on its blinker and slowly came alongside them. The woman said to herself that she had to remain calm, and thought of the first words she would say. Let me do my job, she would say. The car came alongside, and she turned. She glimpsed a face that she didn't know, a young cop. He seemed to be nice enough. He stared at her for a moment and then raised his thumb to ask if everything was all right. She smiled and made the same gesture. The car accelerated, and when it was twenty yards ahead got back in the lane. The woman knew exactly what was happening in that car. One of the two was saying something about the strangeness of women who go driving at night. The other would say nothing and this meant that they wouldn't stop, there was no reason to. If she wants to drive at night, let her, he would perhaps have said. She saw them grow distant and she continued to drive in the most disciplined way possible, in order to be forgotten. She thought she had made it when she saw them disappear around one of the rare curves, and then she gripped the wheel with her hands, because she knew how it worked and she wouldn't be surprised to find them stopped along the road, beyond the curve, waiting for her. She glanced at the boy. He was motionless, eyes closed, head leaning to one side of the seat. She said nothing to him and started to take the curve. All right, she said softly. She saw the road stretching ahead in the darkness and the blue light flashing in the distance. She slowed down a little and kept driving until she saw a turnout on the side of the road. She braked and drove into the turnout, stopping with the engine running. She let go of the steering wheel with her fingers. Fuck, she thought. Just listen to that shit heart pounding, she thought; anything frightens me now. She leaned her forehead against the steering wheel and began to cry, in silence. The boy opened his eyes and looked at her, without moving. He wasn't sure how things had ended up. He looked at the road, but there were no blue lights around, only the darkness of before and nothing else. And yet that woman was crying, and in fact now she was really sobbing, rhythmically beating her head against the steering wheel, but softly, without hurting herself. She didn't stop for a while and the boy didn't dare to do anything, until she suddenly raised her head, dried her eyes on the sleeve of her jacket, turned to him and, in a rather cheerful voice said, Just what was needed. The boy smiled.

Something you should learn, Malcolm, is that… your name is Malcolm, right?

Yes.

Well, a thing you should learn, Malcolm, is that when someone needs to cry he should do it, useless to sit there and worry about it.

Yes.

Afterward everything is better.

Yes.

Do you have a handkerchief?

No.

I had one, somewhere… Everything okay?

Yes.

Shall we get going, what do you say?

Okay with me.

Also with me. So off we go.

Do we know where we're going?

Of course.

Where?

Straight ahead, to the sea.

We're going to the *sea*?

There's a friend of mine there. You'll feel good there.

I don't want to go to your friend, I want to stay with you.

He's much better. Stay with him and nothing can happen to you.

Why?

I don't know why. But it's so.

Is he old?

Like me. Two years older. But he's not old—he's not someone who will ever be old. It will be like staying with another child, you'll see.

I don't want to stay with another child. I never am with other children.

All right, I tell you it will be fine, you trust me?

Who is he?

A friend of mine, I told you.

Friend in what sense?

Oh goodness, what do you want to know?

Why him?

Because the only places I know are grim, but with him it's nice, and you need to be in a beautiful place.

Beautiful because there's the sea?

No, beautiful because he's there.

What do you mean?

Oh, Jesus, don't make me explain everything, I'm not capable of explaining to you.

Try.

You're too much.

Come on.

I don't know, it's the only place that came to mind, you were there on that terrible bed in that awful room and the only thing I could think was that I couldn't leave you there, so I asked myself if there was a place to take you that was the most beautiful place in the world, and the truth is that I don't know the most beautiful places in the world, I don't have any anywhere, except for one, or maybe two, counting the gardens of Barrington Court, I don't know if you've ever seen them, but except for those, which are too far, I only know one most beautiful place in the world, because I was there, and I know that it is truly the most beautiful place in the world, so I thought that I would be able take you there if only I could drive for hours at night, it's a thing I hate doing and just to think about it causes me anguish, but looking at you while you tried to go to sleep I decided that I would be capable of it, and that's why I got you up and put you in the car, having decided that I would manage to take you to him, because the things around him and the way he has of touching them and of talking about them are the most beautiful place in the world, the only one I have. Do I have to repeat, putting the sentences in better order?

No, I understand.

Good.

If it's so beautiful why don't you live there?

There, now we're starting the interrogation again. You'd go far in the police, you know?

Just tell me that. Why don't you live there, if he is… if it's so beautiful there.

It's a story for grown-ups, forget it.

Tell me just the beginning.

The beginning, what beginning?

How the story begins.

You're something.

Please.

It's nothing, the usual story, he's the man of my life and I'm the woman of his life, that's it, except that we have never been able to live together. Satisfied?

Thank you.

It's not necessarily true that if you really love someone, really a lot, the best thing you can do together is *live*.

No?

Not necessarily.

Oh.

I warned you it was something for grown-ups.

Yes, you warned me.

You'll like him. Him. You'll like him.

Maybe.

You'll see.

What does he do?

Boats. Small wooden boats. He makes them one by one, he spends all his time thinking about his boats. They're beautiful.

He makes them himself?

From top to bottom, everything.

And then?

He sells them. Every so often he gives them as gifts. He's crazy.

Did he ever give you one?

Me? No. But once he made one with my name. He wrote it in eleven secret places, and no one will ever know, except me.

And me.

And you, now.

Nice.

He promised me, and then he did it.

Nice.

Yes. Oh lord, every so often I wonder what sort of creep must have that boat now, and I'm no longer sure that it's such a beautiful story.

You don't know where your boat is.

No.

Ask him.

Him?

Yes.

No way. I don't want to know anything about him and his boats, the less I know, the better off I am.

I'll ask him, then.

Don't even try.

Did you tell him what happened to me?

Him? No.

He doesn't know anything?

For that matter, he doesn't even know we're coming.

You didn't tell him.

No. I didn't feel like telephoning him. I haven't called him for a long time.

But really…

In fact, to tell the truth, it's been a long time since I've seen him.

How long?

I don't know. Two, three years. Dates aren't my strong point.

Two or three years?

Something like that.

And you didn't even let him know you were going there?

I never do. I arrive and I ring the bell; every time it's happened I arrived and rang the bell. And he, once, came to my house and rang the bell. We don't like to telephone.

Maybe he's not even there.

Possible.

And what do we do if he's not there?

Look how marvelous.

What?

The light, over there. It's called dawn.

Dawn.

Exactly. We've made it, kiddo.

And in fact from the horizon rose a crystalline light that revived everything and set time in motion again. Maybe it was the reflection on the sea, in the distance, but there was something metallic in the air that not every dawn has, and the woman thought this would help her to remain lucid and calm. It wasn't something to tell the boy, but in fact returning after all that time made her anxious. Besides, she knew she didn't have another plan, if that one failed, which might also happen. Maybe he wasn't there. Maybe he was with a woman, or with who knows. There were plenty of ways in which the whole thing could go wrong. Yet she imagined the way in which, on the other hand, it could go very right, and she knew that in that case she couldn't have invented anything better for the boy, about that she had no doubts. It was just a matter of remaining optimistic. The light helped her. So she began to laugh, with the boy, telling him some stories of when she was a child. At some point they found the popcorn. Driving now was easier, and not even the fact that she had been driving for hours weighed on her anymore. They reached the sign for the city almost before they knew it. The woman stopped the car and got out to stretch her legs. The boy also got out. He said that the city had a nice name. Then he said he had to pee and he went into the fields. In the middle of that horizon of grass and distant houses, he looked small to the woman, and she felt a pang that she didn't understand, it was so difficult to separate the flavor of regret from the good feeling of having done something worthwhile. Maybe you're not the failure you think you are after all, she said to herself. And for a second there returned to her the silvery impudence she'd had when she was young, when she knew she was neither worse nor better than many others, but only different, in a precious and inevitable way. It was when everything scared her, but she wasn't yet scared of anything. Now that so much time had passed, a kind of uneasy weariness had taken hold of everything, and the clarity of that feeling had become rare. She found it there, on the edge of the road, in front of a sign that bore a name, that name, and she hoped that it wouldn't vanish immediately. She had a strong desire for it to stay with her until they arrived, because then the man would read it in her eyes and again would think how singular she was, and beautiful, and unique. She turned because the boy was shouting something to her. She couldn't hear clearly, but he pointed to the horizon, and then she looked, and what she saw was a truck, standing out in the metallic dawn light, hauling a boat, amid the fields, a large white boat that seemed to plow a ridiculous path through the corn, its sails lowered and the rudder facing the hills. Let's go, she shouted to the boy. She looked at the time and thought it might be a little early to show up there, by surprise, but when the boy arrived she got in the car and started the engine because she had some force in herself and she didn't know how long it would last. It didn't matter if they woke him up, she thought, he wasn't the type to get mad. It didn't even matter if she found him with a woman, at that moment it seemed to her that it wouldn't matter much. She had been like that, so long ago, as a girl.

They crossed the center of the city and then took a dirt road that led to the sea. They entered a small open space surrounded by low, bright-colored houses and glided slowly amid skeletons of boats and engines. They stopped in front of a one-story house, painted red and white. The woman turned the engine off. Let's go, she said. But she didn't move. The boy looked at her without knowing what to do. With a caress she rumpled his black hair and said it would all be fine. She was saying it to herself, and the boy understood. Yes, he said.

At the door there was a small bronze bell, of the type that are usually on boats, and the woman pulled the chain and let it ring a couple of times. It had a nice crystalline sound. For a while nothing happened, then the door opened.

The man was in a T-shirt and boxers, his feet bare. Disheveled gray hair.

Hello, Jonathan, the woman said.

You, the man said simply, as if answering a question. Then he turned to look at the boy. He did it with his eyes half-closed, because he wasn't yet used to the morning light.

This is Malcolm, the woman said.

The man examined him for a moment. Then he turned to look at the woman.

Is he mine? he asked.

The woman didn't understand right away.

Is he by chance a son of mine? the man said, calmly.

The woman burst out laughing.

What the hell are you talking about, he's a boy, that's all, do you think I would have hidden a son of yours for thirteen years?

You're very capable of it, the man said, but still calmly. Then he took a step toward the boy and held out his hand. Hello, Mark, he said. You're rather small to go around with such beautiful women, he said. Look out, he added.

Malcolm, not Mark, said the woman.

Then they went into the house and the man began to prepare breakfast. There was a single big room, full of objects, which served as a kitchen and living room. Somewhere there must be a bedroom. The woman knew where things were, and started to set the table. What she had imagined was exactly that, a breakfast made for the boy on a carefully laid table. Meanwhile she told a little of the story, but not all of it. The man listened without interrupting and every so often he gave the boy something to do, as if they weren't talking about him. You should keep him here a few days, the woman said, just until his uncle arrives from the North. A few days, she repeated.

Of course, the man said. There was a delicious smell of French toast.

Only when they had eaten and cleaned up everything the woman said she really had to go. She went to the car to get the boy's things, the jacket and the other things, and put everything on the sofa, in the house. She simply shook the boy's hand, because she was a detective, and gave some orders that made him smile.

Keep an eye on him, from time to time, she said in a low voice. He can make messes that you can't imagine.

She and the man parted without saying anything, a kiss on the lips. Just a little long—and he closed his eyes.

She got in the car, first brushing the popcorn off the seat. She buckled the seat belt, but then she sat there, without turning on the engine. She looked at the house in front of her, and thought of the mysterious permanence of things in the unceasing current of life. She was thinking that, living with them, one always leaves on them a sort of thin coat of paint, the color of certain emotions destined to fade under the sun, in memories. She was also thinking that she would have to get gas and retrace that whole road, by herself, and it would be a colossal pain. At least it's not dark, she said to herself. Then she saw the door of the house open and the man came out, still in a T-shirt and bare feet, walking slowly toward her. He stopped next to the car door. The woman turned the key and lowered the window, but not completely. He placed a hand on it.

The wind is right, he said. Maybe we could go out on the bay.

The woman said nothing. Her eyes were fixed on the house.

You'll leave tonight, what will happen? said the man.

Then the woman turned to him and saw the same face she had seen so many other times, the crooked teeth, the pale eyes, the boyish lips, the hair spiky on his head. It took her a while to say something. She was thinking of the mysterious permanence of love, in the unceasing current of life.

ALESSANDRO BARICCO is an Italian writer, director, and performer. He has won the Prix Médicis Étranger in France and the Selezione Campiello, Viareggio, and Palazzo al Bosco prizes in Italy.

ANN GOLDSTEIN is an editor at the *New Yorker*. She has translated works by, among others, Pier Paolo Pasolini, Alessandro Baricco, Romano Bilenchi, and Elena Ferrante. She is currently editing the Complete Works of Primo Levi in English, and has been the recipient of a PEN Renato Poggioli translation award and a Guggenheim Fellowship.